EBURY

WHERE THE SU

Stuti Changle is a bestselling author. Her books *You Only Live Once* and *On the Open Road* have inspired readers across the country to make a move.

Stuti quit her job to inspire people by sharing life-changing stories. She made her TV debut in 2019 as a host of the series *Kar Ke Dikhaenge*.

She currently divides her time between India and the US, where she lives with her husband, Kushal Nahata, co-founder and CEO of FarEye.

She loves to connect with her readers. Talk to her on
Instagram: @stutichangle
Facebook: stutichangle1
Twitter: Stutichangle

To stay updated on events, book tours, speaking engagements, storytelling workshops, readers' meet and greet, press releases and blog posts, log on to www.stutichangle.com.

Make a move!
Lots of love,
Stuti

ALSO BY THE AUTHOR

On the Open Road: 3 Lives 5 Cities 1 Dream

You Only Live Once: One for Passion. Two for Love.
Three for Friendship

Where the Sun Never Sets

STUTI CHANGLE

Bestselling author of *You Only Live Once*

EBURY PRESS

An imprint of Penguin Random House

EBURY PRESS

USA | Canada | UK | Ireland | Australia
New Zealand | India | South Africa | China

Ebury Press is part of the Penguin Random House group of companies
whose addresses can be found at global.penguinrandomhouse.com

Published by Penguin Random House India Pvt. Ltd
4th Floor, Capital Tower 1, MG Road,
Gurugram 122 002, Haryana, India

First published in Ebury Press by Penguin Random House India 2022

10 9 8 7 6 5 4 3 2 1

ISBN 9780143453673

Typeset in Sabon by Manipal Technologies Limited, Manipal
Printed at Thomson Press India Ltd, New Delhi

www.penguin.co.in

To the desperate times that test
human resilience and eventually teach us to cope,
in our way.

‘Schrödinger’s cat has far more than nine lives, and far fewer. All of us are unknowing cats, alive and dead at once, and of all the might-have-beens in between, we record only one.’

—Yoon Ha Lee, *Conservation of Shadows*

Prologue

It all began on 24 March 2020. Under Prime Minister Narendra Modi, the Government of India ordered a national lockdown that lasted approximately three months, restricting the movement of India's entire population of 1.3 billion. It was a protective measure against the Covid-19 pandemic.

On 2 June 2020, I woke up to 2020's biggest fear—a family member testing positive for Covid-19 and the inability to be with them due to the lockdown. I received a call at 9 a.m., and my mom told me that she had tested positive and that a team of six people had entered my parents' apartment in the city of Indore to sanitize every corner of it. Mind you, these were not the times of vaccinations and clarity. These were the times of no proven treatments and confusion.

In the week following this, I wrote a blog post that went viral and helped many people get a much-needed dose of positivity against this unknown monster. But what many people don't know is how daunting it was for me to live for a month in the constant fear of losing my mother. On most nights, I was anxious, depressed and besieged by hopelessness.

In fact, when she finally tested negative after a month, I could not travel to Indore for a few more months as Covid-19 cases had started exploding, with the maximum cases being reported by July end. I feared becoming a carrier and the possibility of her or any other family member contracting the infection.

Those months were some of the most challenging times of my life, even if they were pretty unique too. My second book, *You Only Live Once*, topped the charts, but on the other hand, I realized that the only thing that would make me happy was being with my mother.

Most of all, I realized that only some people stood by my side during the crisis. I now know that they are the only ones who matter in my life.

A few months after I started working on this book, I contracted Covid-19 in the great Delta wave of India that peaked in April 2021. At the time, vaccinations were not available for people under the age of forty-five in India. I developed moderate symptoms with a fever that lasted for almost ten days. I lost almost seven kilos. Once I started recovering from the disease, it took me months of yoga and meditation to regain my mental health. I lost some relatives, some friends and some friends of friends. Suddenly, the virus from the 'news' had become the virus of our 'lives'.

I went for therapy to take care of my mental health, and that was probably the first time in my life that I realized how much therapy can help one cope with post-traumatic stress disorder (PTSD).

Writing was the one thing that kept me going even during the darkest time of my life.

Life tests you, challenges you and sometimes changes you as a person. These defining moments of my life have to be shared; the story needs to be told.

This novel is my tribute to that time of my life. This novel is a tribute to those years of the pandemic when each one of us faced our share of difficulties and challenges. When we lost jobs, family members, people we loved and even the will to survive.

This novel is a salute to the human spirit of never giving up and finding hope in the darkest of times.

I wrote this novel as a coping mechanism. It is a work of fiction and therefore has been dramatized to some extent. But writing this book helped me heal.

I believe that it will help you heal too!

Here's my mother's story as published in the *Times of India*: https://timesofindia.indiatimes.com/home/sunday-times/five-covid-19-survivors-share-their-recovery-stories/articleshow/77155134.cms

Acknowledgements

I would like to thank my readers who make me live my dream.

Kushal Nahata, my old-friend-turned-annoying-husband, for believing in me and my love for storytelling—today and forever.

Mom and Dad, for bringing me into this world and not abandoning me despite my unconventional career choice. Swapnil Changle, for being there by my side through thick and thin. My dreams would not have seen the light of day without your love.

My friends for always being there for me.

My fans from the social media community for encouraging me to do more.

Disclaimer

Hey you!

You must be sitting at home, or sipping coffee in a café, or stalking your ex, or lying on the beach. There is a multitude of things you could be doing when you find my diary.

And in case you've done so, let me tell you a little about me.

I write scripts for digital advertisements as my day job. My purpose quite clearly is to feed off people's insecurities, not unlike a blood-sucking parasite. Though I work in a white-collar day job, I am not a monk in a red robe. I know that well, but I don't have an option. It's the money I make that fuels my existence, and my desire to be the coolest in any group that I hang out with that drives my life decisions.

I sell fairness creams to brown-skinned people, magic hair oils to bald people, fat-free cooking oil to heart patients, dishwashing gels with real lemon and real juices with artificial flavours.

Have you ever accidentally switched on your not-so-smart TV in the morning and come across teleshopping ads? One of those shouting buffoons is my neighbour, Virjee. To earn money, one has to do all sorts of shit. Thankfully, I am not one of those presenters who sells abominable stuff through ads. It is always more comfortable to write lies than to speak them. Nobody can look into your eyes and bust you. I can't lie with my eyes wide open. But my older sister, Riti, is different. She can lie to your face without batting an eyelash. She's so manipulative that you can never tell what is going on in her life.

'We sell dreams,' my boss always says. I do as he says. Mostly. When you work in advertising you find yourself living in a world of lies. That makes you a pessimist. I am anything but hopeful about this earth. You know how they cringe about doomsday? If you work in advertising, you know that it's already here.

My colleagues buy vegan, cruelty-free products but eat chicken soup for dinner. They talk about body positivity in front of everyone but deep within believe that most overweight people are lethargic and addicted to junk. They avoid the sun for fear of getting darker but consume laboratory-manufactured vitamin D supplements. Their Facebook page displays pictures that say 'Black Lives Matter' and therefore they get their hair coloured if they see the slightest bit of grey. They don't consume fruits, only canned juices with preservatives, and their hair is full of laboratory-synthesized keratin.

They buy every lie sold to them.

When I talk to my boss about this, he laughs and says, 'As long as people are insecure, kiddo, you and I will mint a lot of money. Their insecurities are our strength.'

I am not a social media influencer but stalk people who have so-called perfect lives for momentary happiness. I am a liar; I am an opportunist, too.

See, I am an advertising professional. I know that a perfect life is a lie, a perfect story is just giving hope! I am raw, unadulterated and real. I am an opportunist at work and a total hypocrite at heart.

I believe each of us is a fool if observed long enough. I believed that kissing a guy could get me pregnant as a thirteen-year-old and here I am, convinced at twenty that even having sex won't if he wears a bloody condom.

I belong to the generation that looks for every answer on Quora or Google. I belong to the generation that looks for entertainment on fifteen-second videos because that's just how long I can feel entertained.

Why are you even reading this? This is not a fifteen-minute read.

I am not always right. Would you believe me? I have made some terrible mistakes in life. Would you still believe me?

I should warn you not to read my diary. It holds my life's biggest secrets. I don't trust you. You might share them with everyone. If you still choose to read further, please do so at your own risk!

I was not always this cynical. I was once a young girl who looked at life through rose-tinted glasses.

Times change and so do we . . .

Yours,
Iti

The Movie

20 March 2020

Dear Diary,

Today was neither the best nor the worst day of my life.

I want to tell you about my life again. I had almost stopped sharing with you. Let me confess, 2019 was the busiest and loneliest year of my life. I hardly had time to spare.

But 2020? It is the scariest! If you were alive in 2020, you mostly googled and looked at graphs of rising Covid-19 cases, and thanked God for not contracting the virus. You did it till you realized that it was pointless to live in fear, confusion and drama forever.

My long-lost friend Shelly told me I must write in my diary when I feel anxious. She told me that friendships last forever. She also told me that love never dies. She told me a lot of things that gave me hope. Shelly was the kind of friend who outperforms you in everything. I always wanted to be her.

She kind of abandoned me later, you know the story. But her life advice never sucked.

So here I am, pouring my thoughts out to you afresh!

After all that happened in 2016, I never wanted to return to my hometown. But I have finally come home for the first time after 2016. I was quite scared about the surprises that awaited me.

Nevertheless, fasten your seat belts like I did. I drove at 100 mph on the highway. I didn't fear falling into the valley as I navigated sharp turns on the mountains. I have matured enough to appreciate that death is the ultimate, only life is penultimate.

And I do feel like my life is taking a turn. For better or worse? Only time will tell.

There is an inexplicable rush in travelling on the road that leads home, an unsettling quest to conquer more on the way back. I was in my new Jazz car, en route to Mussoorie from Gurgaon via Delhi, Roorkee and Dehradun.

Today marked my longest drive on the highway. It was such a thrill. Can you believe I drove 290 km—with my colleague Riddhima—but did not make even one stop, for fear of contamination? I pray to God for the Covid-19 pandemic to disappear in a few days, but right now, it's on a path to take over the world.

I started work at a top advertising firm, W&W, in Gurgaon. You see, there is so much news to share. So much has happened since 2018 when I last poured out my overwhelming thoughts to you.

Writing jingles and dialogues for TV commercials and part-time copywriting for social media ads is now my thing. Two years into fooling people to buy fairness creams and fat-free cooking oils, I believed I had aced the game. That not even God could stop my promotion. Until my big fat boss, Kajol, called me up the other day.

Kajol sounds sane on most days. He never asks me to venture into the impossible. But on that day, he was not himself.

Kajol's boss, Prakash, my grandfather—yes, you've got me right—is quite entrepreneurial. He sensed the upcoming lockdown and figured out that theatres were going to shut. There would be a massive demand for scripts for over the top (OTT) platforms. He asked Kajol to put the best copywriter from his team to work on writing a script for a movie for his latest acquisition, LightSpeed, a production company.

I was the chosen one. I never say I am the best. I just try my best.

Kajol felt I was the best fit for the job. When he felt so, suddenly, so did I. You can avoid your dad for any number of reasons, but you can't mess with your grandfather. He is your gateway to extra pocket money!

Unfortunately, Covid-19 emerged as a global pandemic that left some world leaders wailing for their countries, and many running for their lives. The government has advised against movement from 24 March onwards. Exactly four days from now.

Trust me, diary. I have heard about the state of emergency that was declared in India back in the 1970s. I have heard about a virus that wiped out the entire Native American population when Christopher Columbus discovered the Americas. I have read stories about the gigantic ship *Titanic* that sank in the Atlantic Ocean claiming the lives of many. But the kind of confusion and drama that surrounds Covid-19 is one of a kind. I have not seen anything of this sort in my life.

My boss asked me to work on the script from my hometown, Mussoorie. And it made sense as travel fuels creativity.

At least, my favourite blogger, Ramy, vouches for that. I wish he knew I have many reasons to avoid the alleys that lead to the past. You know, though, my diary! But I have come a long way in life, enough to realize that we don't run away from places, we run away from people. Most of them would have moved out of Mussoorie over the past few years. So, I didn't have a lot to fear, and when I was presented with the opportunity to go back, I did not complain.

I also wanted to be with my memories, with Mom and Dad for some time. The whole situation felt like a blessing in disguise. After graduating from college, I didn't have the chance to go back home. Do you remember?

I started my career with an internship that I got when I was in the third year of my mass communication course. It was at a news blog in Bangalore, writing articles about anything from start-ups to suicide. But that was never my calling.

I have always wanted to write a script. Especially for a movie.

'Isn't working from home scary?' Riddhima interrupted as I was lost in thought. 'You can't have a professional environment,' she added. 'I am certainly going to miss our masala chai sessions.'

'Your parents won't be home. They are government officials and might need to visit the office on some days. I guess I should be more scared!' I replied.

'Oh yes! Your parents must be retired and will be at home all the time. You are going to miss the freedom of city life,' she said with a sly grin.

It's interesting how people sometimes assume everything about you but in reality know nothing about you. I chose not to reply and let her believe her version of the story. There is no absolute truth. We all live in our version of reality. We all want to tell our side of the story.

She stretched her left arm out of the window, feeling the wind. I wanted to do that, too, but I was driving.

'Given there will be an absolute lockdown, I'm not sure if we can even escape to the terrace.' I smiled, increasing the volume of the stereo. My sentence was as unnecessary as the icing on a cake. You know how much I hate cream, my diary. I am a brownie person.

'You bet! You live in the outskirts, though. You should be able to cheat,' she said. 'Do you have any ideas?' she asked me as she moved her fingers in a circular motion through her hair as if she were massaging her head.

'About?' I got curious.

'The movie script you're supposed to write!'

'No. Honestly. Since it's the first time that I'm going to write a movie script, I am rather nervous and keep having fleeting thoughts and ideas,' I blurted out as I trembled deep within, scared that the news might spread like wildfire in the office. She already knew about my deal with our boss.

'Oh, I see. I am a little nervous as well.' She kept massaging her head.

'About what? You're sorted. You have your fixed set of things to deliver. Some copy-editing, some client management, some calls. Plus, no client is going to put in an extra budget during the lockdown. Only essentials like groceries are going to sell,' I replied.

'Some apparel brands are going to come up with fashionable masks soon. I guess we need to be ready for those jingles. I overheard the accounts guy say that IndiRetail has a big mask campaign planned,' she said.

'Could be. But I'm free of all this. It will be directed towards you,' I said with a chuckle.. I was the chosen one after all.

'Umm . . . actually, I guess you don't know, but even I have been asked to work on a script.' She seemed a little surprised that I did not know about this.

'What?' I said, sharp and loud. A truck overtook us. 'Idiot,' I shouted. The driver sped along the unending highway, the back of his truck flaunting in big bold letters, '*Samay se pehle bhagya se zyada kisiko nahi milta* [You never get more than your destiny or before the destined time]!' Who knows this better than you, my diary? I always have to walk the extra mile to get anything I set my heart on.

I was not the chosen one.

Riddhima's words combined with the wisdom on that Haryana Roadways truck felt like a slap across my face. I will have to work hard to see that my movie gets to the screen. Our boss must have asked many colleagues to work on the script.

'I guess they're going to have a look at the options and pick the best one,' she reaffirmed that my aspirations were misplaced.

'Oh! I see. They are making us work on something for the sake of our salaries. Since most of our clients won't be putting in budgets. How mean is that!' I retorted.

'At least it's better than being fired. I heard that the new batch is going to be laid off. Some people from our batch have also been laid off.' She paused and added, 'It's an opportunity for us to move ahead in our careers. We should take it positively. I don't know about you, but I think writing ad jingles now kind of sucks.'

'I am looking at the bright side,' I pretended with a smile like a calm monk in a red robe. But I get furious when I lose a ludo game. How would I find the peace to finish my story?

We travelled as the dawn made way for the sun and the dusk made way for the moon. The landscape with almost no greenery on either side of the road changed to sparse forests of sal trees and then to dense forests of deodar trees. The straight road soon became a sinuous one with the mountains on one side and the valley on the other. The suffocating smell of the city smog was replaced by the sublime smell of the forest. The country music that played in the car during the rest of the drive saved me from having any more awkward conversations with Riddhima.

It is at times like these when I miss my family. It is at times like these when I miss Nishit and Shelly. The mountains remind me of the people I love. You make really good friends at school but sometimes fail to keep them. You try to befriend a lot of colleagues but sometimes fail to let them go. You believe that your colleagues might one day metamorphose from caterpillars into butterflies. But sooner or later you realize that the butterflies you failed at holding when they were close will never return to your life.

I looked at Riddhima. I felt nothing. That's the thing with colleagues. No matter how many hours you spend with them, they are not friends. That's one of the reasons why you feel disillusioned every time you're hit with the reality of city life. You're always lonely, looking for family and friends.

But I have you, my diary. Keeping you is the closest thing to having a butterfly. In your embrace, my heart flutters and opens up.

We left at 6 a.m. and at 7 p.m., we made a stop at her apartment which is 7 km before mine. She lives quite close to the Mussoorie library. You know, my diary, I have such fond memories of that place.

We bid each other goodbye with a fake promise to keep in touch during the lockdown and share ideas on the movie script. Deep within, we both knew that we would next meet only after the lockdown was lifted.

I parked my car in Dad's garage; 'Sujay's garage' was written in bold black letters on one of the walls. That's another thing about moving back home. I suddenly felt that I was a princess who had moved back to her castle, given that my family owns a huge bungalow in Mussoorie. Just the garage and outhouse are bigger than my studio apartment in Gurgaon. I feel the 'studio' in 'studio apartment' is only as good as the delusion provided by 'happily' in 'happily married'. My studio apartment in Gurgaon is a rat hole but quite tastefully done up with cheap furnishings that I found on the Big Billion Day sale.

But everything comes at a cost. Sometimes, individual freedom comes at the cost of relationships. Sometimes, staying cloistered comes at the cost of a fancy city life.

My elder sister Riti's apartment could be anything; she has never invited me over, so I don't have a clear picture of it. Sometimes, keeping up with her, the arrogant elder sister, feels like paying off a loan I never applied for! Too much responsibility. It is for the sake of Mom and Dad that I have not given up on her yet.

Do you know, diary, how we were all christened?

Dad was a scientist, you see. When he couldn't name Mom Andromeda—after one of his favourite galaxies—during their wedding rituals, they agreed upon letting him name her Akkriti, which means shape. Then the kids followed. My sister was named Riti, which means custom, and I am Iti, which means the end. He felt that I was everything they needed to complete the family. But Jay was born only two years after me. 'Jay' is also the latter part of Dad's name, Sujay.

Our names follow this thought, like a sequence, taking some letters out to arrive at the next name. Dad named my golden retriever Corona. His name was inspired by something to do with the sun's envelope during a total solar eclipse, and not the coronavirus that later became such a threat. A corona around the sun might have existed years before the coronavirus, but 'corona' will be remembered primarily as the coronavirus in history lessons. It's funny in a sad way.

Dad's quest to escape the city in search of land far off where there was no light pollution had always led to trouble. But he was so passionate about astronomy that he wanted us to see the Milky Way with our naked eyes at least once in our lives. So, he asked us to pack our bags and took us to the hills around Mussoorie where we camped under the stars, and he taught us the basic concepts of astronomy.

As I moved past the garage, rang the doorbell and Shyamala Aunty opened the door, reality struck me harder than ever before.

I joined my hands in namaste and bowed in front of the pictures hung just inside the door. Fresh garlands of marigold and bel leaves embraced the black picture frames. Then I read 'Sujay' again, but this time the next word I read wasn't garage but Akkriti. It was also preceded by the word 'Late'.

Dad had always wondered why it was so hard for me to understand physics. But today, entering my home felt like entering a black hole of memories. He'd have appreciated the kind of parallels I can draw between physics and my real life. I understand physics much better now.

Having spent my entire life in Mussoorie, everything reminds me of something. Hometowns cast this weird spell on you. They make you see eternity in a moment. They make you feel the range of emotions you've experienced in a lifetime, in a moment. They make you see flashes of uncountable unclear pictures from the past, in a moment.

The year 2016 flashed all over again in front of my eyes.

Corona, my pet dog, jumped in joy. He almost started wailing because he couldn't believe his nose when he realized it was me. I had come back home after almost four years.

Shyamala Aunty had tears of joy too.

'Is Riti also coming?' she enquired.

'No, I have not heard from her in a long time,' I replied, short and crisp, with no emotion on my face.

'Everyone has to find their way back home once in their lives. I am glad that the pandemic made you find yours. I am certain someday Riti will also find her way back home,' Shyamala Aunty said as she wiped her eyes with the pallu of her beige cotton saree. I noticed her thinning hair and that almost eighty per cent of it had gone grey. Time had moved, indeed.

But coming face to face with the fact that the house would no longer echo with the laughter of my mom and the wisdom of my dad made my limbs stone cold.

My home is a beautiful abode that was done up first by its previous owner and then by my mom. It's a huge, British-style wooden cottage with glimpses of India's colonial past.

My mom wasn't very fond of the absence of colour in our colonial-style home. Mandala art and Jaipuri sheets that she brought back from trips to Rajasthan were proof that India was independent.

The courtyard in front of the cottage is vast and has a lush garden maintained by Shyamala Aunty. It houses an outhouse on one side and Corona's kennel on the other. Shyamala Aunty's cottage is diagonally opposite. It is a gated residence amidst the hills, with grey stone walls forming its boundary.

Tall Victorian-style lamps are omnipresent in the cottage as well as the courtyard. If a faint-hearted person were to arrive at my home, it would certainly remind them of a haunted house.

There are two bedrooms adjacent to the living area and kitchen. The third bedroom was always the kids' room and is on the first floor with a small terrace next to it. The bedroom is like an attic.

I spent my childhood with Riti Didi and Jay in this attic. We had three single beds placed next to each other, separated by a distance of two feet. We had three study tables on the other side of the attic placed similarly. And then our cupboards standing in the same fashion on the other side.

I had been in constant touch with Shyamala Aunty. She knew about my arrival and had joined the three beds to form a larger-than-king-sized bed. She had joined the tables and cupboards too.

As a kid, I had wanted to be my parents' only child because I felt that all their love and attention would be showered on me. It's kind of true now. But I hate my current situation. I would've preferred a happy family to stay with through the lockdown. The mere thought of spending my days as a recluse in the hills fuels my anxiety.

As I entered the attic and arranged my things to prepare for my stay of God knows how long, the memory of a conversation between Mom and Dad resurfaced.

When I was in the seventh standard, we went for a school trip to Shimla. It was the first time I had left home for so many days without my parents.

When I got home after the trip, Mom and Dad had rushed out to hug me. 'I have prepared your favourite bhindi masala,' Mom said.

'With too much oil and salt that can make one unwell,' Dad interrupted.

'Better than not having prepared for our daughter's arrival at all,' Mom shot back and added, 'Just because you have high blood pressure it doesn't mean we all have to eat like patients.' And with that, she left for the kitchen.

Even after many years of marriage, they continued to fight like kindergarteners. Their marriage was as everlastingly pure as the promise on a bottle of glacier water. However, at that moment, I had felt reassured that everything was fine at home. Had they not got into a tiff, I would have smelt danger.

They would often tease each other. The only thing that scared me was one of them falling prey to Alzheimer's and forgetting all the mistakes of the other. If that had happened, I might have had to depend on the TV for my entertainment.

Which is kind of true now.

Settling anew in my old home, I started to read about our galaxy. You know, my diary, I have this weird habit of reading anything under the sun. Above the sun. And about the sun. Especially because it reminds me of Dad. If he is watching over me as a guardian angel, he would smile at my new-found passion.

Don't have much else to share. That's all for now. Good night!

Love you,

Iti

The Library

21 March 2020

Dear Diary,

Today felt just like every day is going to feel in my lockdown life.

Once upon a time, it rained for hours, just like it rained today, heavily, unendingly, unstoppably. Rain might wash the physical world, but with it, washed-out memories resurface. Rains deepen the colours of your surroundings as if you've unknowingly switched to 4K HD mode. It also deepens the colours in your mind, unlocking the deepest of desires.

Rain is powerful indeed. And what does rain remind you of?

The rain reminded me of the onion fritters Mom would deep fry until they were golden and crisp. The mere thought lit up my face, filling my mouth with water. I closed my eyes for a moment, imagining the crisp fritters between my teeth, chewing them with a crunch. Nishit, my ex-boyfriend, would often give me company. He would also tell me that peacocks teach you to dance your sorrows away in the rain.

The rain also reminded me of masala chai, the kind my landlady prepares in Gurgaon, with ginger, lemongrass and basil leaves added in generous amounts. She is the kind of bitch who calls you up to catch up and when you do so, she gives you a list of things you need to get repaired at your own expense. She keeps reminding me that I am an orphan and it's her responsibility to bully me to make me stronger. She believes that my parents would have done the same. She also feels that my elder sister is a bitch to have abandoned me. When I am engaged in bitter conversations with her, masala tea is my guru who preaches finding goodness in everything.

I requested Shyamala Aunty to prepare masala tea and fritters in the morning. I gave her very specific instructions.

These days of lockdown have to be the perfect time for me to finish the movie script.

But where to start? Why can't you talk, my diary?

I entered my attic-style bedroom to start writing the script. I had asked Shyamala Aunty to set up my desk in front of the huge window that overlooks the beautiful Mussoorie hills. It's going to be a long lockdown after all.

I watched some YouTube videos by Tibetan Zen masters. They say that one must prepare well before a new project. Some changes are necessary while some are not as important. But the room where you engage in creative work has to be organized.

Considering the lockdown situation, all I can say is that it is one of the most unpredictable times. Of course, things will change sooner or later. They must. That's the hope, and we hang on to it.

But I don't know how much peace organizing my room will bring me when the world is in chaos.

'Relax. Focus. Concentrate. Yes. Harder,' I told myself. 'Write a few words at a time. Bricks build castles. And castles stand for ages and inspire people for many years to come,' I murmured.

I have switched off my smartphone and put it aside. Dad, who was smarter than the smartphones, used to say, 'You should not fall prey to the fear of missing out. The fun is in missing out! Why do you want to be connected with so many people all the time? Why do you have to say yes to every party? Why do you have to stalk your friends' so-called wonderful lives on social media? Why do you have to be the first one to like the pictures of the celebrity you are crushing on? Why don't you have some real goals in life? Beyond social media?'

I sat at my desk wondering if all the days were going to be the same here. You watch the sunrise. The sunset. Sunrise. Sunset. Yet you feel you're stationary.

'The sunrise. The sunset,' I murmured as I had still not written a single word. I put my pen aside.

'Time never really moves here. That's the beauty of time in small towns,' Shyamala Aunty said, breaking my reverie.

I hadn't realized she had entered the room. She sneaks in whenever she likes, and I have hated it since my teenage years.

She continued to mop the floor with a magic mop, even as its engineering was beyond her comprehension.

It reminded me of my arguments with Dad, who often said, 'It is important for everyone to understand mathematics to be able to lead a good life.'

I would always tell him, 'It is not important to understand an airplane's engineering to be able to travel in it. You could be a layman and still live a happy life.'

I turned to Shyamala Aunty and said, 'Time is unimportant in a place where there's nothing to do. You've spent your entire life as a recluse! You never agreed to move out and stay with me in Gurgaon.' I let out a sarcastic laugh.

'But I love my life here. I feel my kids, Shonu-Monu, are safe here in the hills,' she replied with a pleasant smile. She's annoying beyond belief at times.

'Here? There are no opportunities to grow here. You've spent years taking care of this home. No ambition. No desire. Limited social circle. I have sympathy for you. How could you even breathe here for a second after all that happened in 2016?' I looked helplessly out of the window.

'Where do I have to grow? My children are happy. Your parents left enough land and a farm for me to take care of. I feel lucky that I was born in such a good place and met such a nice family that feels like my own. I have seen in the news that there are so many robberies, murders, rapes and whatnot in the city.' She continued to clean my room. I felt like offering a helping hand but held myself back.

'There isn't a mobile tower in the entire area. We live on the outskirts of the town. The network can't support video calls even through Wi-Fi,' I screamed like a child. I don't know what happens to me when I return home. I forget that I am an independent person now. I behave, or rather misbehave, like a ten-year-old kid. Shyamala Aunty has been handling my tantrums as my mother would have.

'We have lots of trees, farms, lovely dogs and cows. This is a clean town, unlike the rest of India. We never leave our community, you see, so we don't need the phone. We're there in person, in good times and bad times alike. Isn't it bliss?' she asked me with a patient smile.

'It is so boring here. I am not getting any ideas to work on! I thought it would be the opposite when I was on my way here,' I yelled in frustration. I had never wanted to return to Mussoorie.

Why haven't they launched daily flights to Mars yet? You know, my diary, I would be the first one to leave earth.

'No noise. No traffic. No pollution. Isn't this what a beautiful life should look like? It should also stimulate a creative mind,' Shyamala Aunty pressed her point.

'Yet, all I want is to run away. Run back to normal civilization. My colleagues. My life,' I told her. I didn't want her to live under the impression that I had returned to Mussoorie forever.

'You never should have left them in the first place,' she said with a meek smile. 'But don't worry, the pandemic will be over soon, and you can drive back. You own a car now, big girl.'

'Is there anything you can say to make my mood better?' I asked her with a forced smile.

'We're cut off so we can't contract Covid-19. You will live. No matter what. Isn't that something to celebrate?' She is too stubborn not to believe that we are having the time of our lives. Feels like God slipped datura pills in her morning tea.

'Hmm! Can you suggest some story ideas?' I thought why not ask the only adult around.

'There's inspiration all around. Go and work in your uncle Nick's library. Read good books. Write about your life. People relate to real-life incidents.'

'Not a bad idea,' I said.

'History repeats itself. It happened back then too. It happened during the war,' Shyamala Aunty mumbled.

'War?' I got curious for the first time.

'Yes. During the war and emergency, people went through this lockdown kind of situation. My nani used to tell us bedtime stories when we were young.'

'Oh yes! Maybe I can write a story that moves back and forth between the war and the lockdown . . . Thanks!' I had just found my first idea for the movie.

'Your uncle Nick was fond of books. There are a lot of books in the outhouse library. Many anthropologists, historians, researchers, writers and tourists quench their thirst for knowledge there when they come to live with us as paying guests.'

'Sometimes experiences are better than books. Humans survived on stories long before they had a knack for facts,' I replied.

'You're a big girl now. You can figure things out for yourself,' she said as she left the room, which she was done cleaning.

We've been lucky with this house. Have I ever shared the story with you, diary?

My late maternal uncle Nick got the cottage from an Englishman in exchange for one of his exquisite paintings. Uncle Nick was an artist and worked in the outhouse. He was a true non-conformist. My cousins told me he was gay and therefore never married. I wish

I had met him. But he hanged himself in the outhouse and that's why I don't wish to work there.

He passed on this property to my mother, and she transformed it into a beautiful home with a beautiful library-cum-art exhibition in his outhouse.

The hills surrounding the cottage are beyond beautiful. If I had a way with words as Shakespeare did, I would still be unable to describe them in a way that did them justice. The lush greenery explodes along the roads. The nights are beyond comparison.

There's a reason the English used these hills for their summer residences. My home is no less than a piece of heritage and a reminder of India's colonial past.

Shyamala Aunty entered my room again. 'Should I give you one more piece of advice? It has nothing to do with the film.'

'Go ahead,' I muttered.

'You should change Corona's name. His life is at risk given the rage of people against the virus and pets.' She seemed a little worried, which was unlike her.

She was the kind of woman who could climb Everest and still not complain about the arduous journey, unlike some of my colleagues back in Gurgaon who would order via food delivery apps and complain if they had to walk even a kilometre for groceries! She had to be taken seriously.

'What are you talking about?' I asked her, frowning.

'I saw on the news yesterday that a lot of people are abandoning their pets as a rumour that pets are spreading the coronavirus is doing the rounds,' she explained.

I suddenly realized that fake content on the internet had manipulated someone as calm as her. What era are we living in?

'WhatsApp University,' I said, 'where so many people keep absorbing the wrong knowledge, for all the wrong reasons.'

'I know, beta. But taking care of Corona is our responsibility. The poor speechless animal can't defend himself,' she added, petting Corona. She is the kindest soul I have ever met.

In India, the house help are a more integral part of your family than even your relatives. Shyamala Aunty means that and a lot more to me. We fancy the Western wave of individualism, but in desperate times we realize that all we need is our family, a sense of belonging. Shyamala Aunty means that to me now.

After saying her piece, Shyamala Aunty left my room again. She knows that when I start shouting against the internet I can go on for ages. She had to finish her chores, so she quickly went to the kitchen.

The rumour 'Corona spreading corona' could start at any time, and I didn't want my baby to fall prey to it. Creepy journalists clad in masks will never let the world live in peace, even with the lockdown. Anyway, our colony is quite anti-pets, so I would have to take Corona out for a walk while the world slept.

This could seriously impact my sleep cycle. But creative people work at night, they say. Maybe I will find a magic wand like Harry Potter's and beat the challenges that come my way.

In the meantime, I called up Corona's vet, Dr Paliwal, to ask him if I could change Corona's name.

He explained, 'Dogs don't listen to the entire word. Instead, they register certain frequencies. Try something that sounds similar to Corona.'

'What about Verona?'

'That should be just fine,' he assured me before he hung up.

Verona is also a beautiful place in Italy. It's famous for being the setting for William Shakespeare's classic play *Romeo and Juliet*.

'Verona, I have a sweet biscuit,' I shouted. Corona came running into the room. The trick had worked.

Then I sat down to write.

'No distractions. Focus hard!' I kept telling myself.

I want to write at least one script that will be made into a film. Maybe this one will be my lucky charm. I am an outsider to the film world and it's a tough dream to make true, but I am adamant that one day I will achieve it.

'Can you please come to the kitchen?' Shyamala Aunty called out, breaking my flow again. She had asked me to order cinnamon powder, which is unavailable in the grocery shop where she gets most of our kitchen essentials.

'Cinnamon?' I asked when I reached the kitchen.

'For your favourite smoothie,' she replied.

'I will get it the next time I head out shopping,' I said reluctantly. My laziness knows no bounds when I am back home.

I thought about eating before I started writing. I sat on the counter, next to where Shyamala Aunty was busy cleaning up after preparing breakfast.

I had my favourite masala chai and fritters, then grabbed an apple from the basket on the counter. Corona entered the kitchen.

'Are you hungry, baby?' I asked, cutting a piece of the apple with a knife and holding it out to him. He wagged his tail and finished the piece like a magician skilfully hiding a dove in his jacket.

I love feeding him.

'Will you be okay, memsahib?' Shyamala Aunty asked, worried if I would be able to cope with the memory of my parents

'Don't call me memsahib!' I snapped. India isn't over the post-colonial hangover and is in no mood to get over it any time soon. Plus, I am not my mother. Those words took me back in time at the speed of a rocket. Going back in time is something I don't want to do. I am not very proud of my past, and I want to dedicate my life to building a great future.

'You keep telling me that. But I was taught to address respected members of society in a certain way. You're kind enough to give me respect, but unfortunately, others are not!'

'Call me bro, it's better!'

She laughed, hiding her face in the pallu of her bright orange georgette saree.

'What happened?' I frowned, confused.

'You said bra!' she whispered.

'Bro! Bro is short form for brother,' I explained. She doesn't know these colloquialisms. She hasn't left Mussoorie in her entire life.

'Are you prepared? I gave you extra cash to get all the essentials. Have you stocked up already?' I asked her.

'Yes, I have. But unfortunately, my brother-in-law took half of the money and bought several bottles of alcohol. He worries he might not be able to live without it for so long,' she said gravely.

'Oh my God, Shyamala. You're not supposed to keep in touch with your in-laws. They've never supported you in any way even after your husband passed away. Your brother-in-law can't enter our home. Tell him I will call the police if he ever comes here again,' I scolded her. Sometimes, I feel guilty about scolding the poor soul, but I just couldn't hold myself back. That guy had been threatening her since forever.

'Ok, Memsahib.'

I broke into laughter.

She laughed as well. 'Bro,' she said. 'I have missed you all these years,' she added.

'After all that happened in 2016, I never wanted to come back. Okay, now I am going to work, so please don't bother me. Send lunch to my room,' I said with a smile as fake as the one that the receptionist at the front desk of a five-star hotel gives.

'Okay,' she said as she continued with her chores.

To be honest, I have no idea how one goes about writing an entire story for a film with a fascinating plot and inspiring characters. I only know what I have seen on the YouTube videos I have been watching to learn creative writing and screenwriting.

This wasn't supposed to be my job, but it fascinates me.

Maybe I should have spoken to Shyamala Aunty for longer. She might have the best ideas, you know!

It was still raining. I googled, 'How do you know it is about to rain long before it starts?' and wasted the rest of the day on Quora without writing a single word. Then, I was about to search for Shelly and Nishit on Facebook. But I held myself back. I thought that visiting the past would only aggravate my problems.

I feel upset and guilty about not being able to start on the script. It's the kind of feeling that hits you the day before an exam.

Diary, I am going to go to Uncle Nick's library in the outhouse now. He was ahead of his time, and I am sure that his collection of books will stir my creative side.

Till we meet again,

Iti

The Park

22 March 2020

Dear Diary,

Today I was reminded of the worst year of my life.

I didn't sleep well last night. I don't have any ideas for the script. What do I write about? The challenge is real, and I can't move out from tomorrow onwards. At least, not legally. Where am I going to get ideas now?

Riddhima has a head start of two days. Stupid me!

What could she be writing about? Maybe I should call her and enquire. What do you think, diary? No. It is best not to let your competitor know what you are up to.

If Dad were still alive, he would be working on his latest thesis. It might not have been a good idea to disturb him, either. If Mom were still alive she would be occupied with family Zoom calls throughout the lockdown.

When I think of calling people, there are not many people left in my life that I can call. Is this kind of loneliness worrisome, diary? Would life have been different if I had made different choices in the past? Can you turn the wheel of time to go back and fix your past like the plumber that fixes a leak in a water pipe, diary? Or is it too late and the house is submerged in water and there is no escape from drowning?

Should I call my colleagues, diary? No, I doubt they even have my number saved.

Why can't you talk to me, diary?

I took Verona out for a walk in the morning though. It was after having spent the night in the outhouse, where I had fallen asleep on the sofa by the window that overlooks the blue hills. It was the first rays of the sun at dawn that woke me up.

'Let's go, Verona!' I shouted. Corona wagged his tail and joined me. I put on my mask and we walked towards the community park about a kilometre away from our gated residence.

When we entered the park, I set off at a brisk pace along the cement walkways that form tortuous paths in no specific symmetry, with tall deodar trees on either side of them. In winter, snow covers the entire region, and the park looks like the winter wonderland where Santa Claus comes riding on a sleigh, given its hilly terrain. The government once tried to flatten it out to some extent, but you can't make an ice cream cone look like an ice cream cup.

Since it's almost summer, the snow had long melted. As I walked, some parts of the park were dark under the dense canopy of trees, and the sun had still not figured its way out of the dense fog. Corona started running, wetting some beautiful Victorian-era lamp posts and some trees here and there.

As I pushed myself to exercise, moving faster than a casual walk—something my body does not have time to do in the city—I realized I wasted too much of my life procrastinating over things that matter. A healthy lifestyle was the first. In the hills, it is hard to find another person as unfit as I have become. I weigh eighty kilos and I am just five feet two inches tall. You can imagine my BMI. I am not the most attractive person you can come across. I wear thick spectacles and I had braces.

Shy. Awkward. Lacking confidence. If I had to describe myself as a teenager in three words, these words would suffice. I was conscious of having a wheatish complexion, being hairy and having big teeth. More so because relatives and neighbours constantly judged me. Riti Didi and Jay were the more complimented kids at family functions.

I started reading books early in life because I was a nerd. I was a good performer in school though. I aced at the game of grades.

You know, diary, teenage issues are real and if not resolved, might resurface later. Do you remember, diary, how I've learnt this the hard way?

I was never asked out by a guy, unlike my peers. The only crush I had back in high school, Abhay, never reciprocated my feelings even when he found out that I was madly in love with him. He had a conventionally beautiful, tall and fair girlfriend back then.

In fact, I was so far from being asked out by a guy that most of them would befriend me to get their love messages through to my beautiful friend Shelly.

Diary, you've been my constant love, my biggest support system. I never held back from sharing my pain with you.

The problem was that I believed others' opinions of me. I thought that their perception of me was the ultimate truth. As I grew older, I realized that I was full of talents that many people around me weren't blessed with. I worked hard on them and became the best version of me with every passing day. After all that happened in 2016, I just want to build a successful career and make so much money that everything else becomes unimportant.

I dragged myself, quite literally, after walking just half a kilometre. Faint laughter erupted out of nowhere, the sound growing louder as an athletic guy shot past me.

'Hello,' I shouted, 'I am not a runner like you. I write films. I don't think you can do that. So stop making fun of others.' I suddenly realized, though, that I had not penned a single word of the script yet.

'I'm sorry,' the guy slowed down and glanced back. 'Would you mind taking your mask off?' he asked with a frown.

I knew what he wanted to confirm because the moment he looked back I was sure about it. Isn't it funny how we make decisions based on what we know, while we don't know 98 per cent of it all! I don't know how many million people are in this world, but I had bumped into the only guy I didn't want to.

'Nishit,' I took my mask off. 'What are you doing here?' I said stupidly.

'Iti! What a pleasant surprise. I am here with my family before the lockdown begins—just like you are, I assume,' he said in a level tone.

An awkward silence hung between us for a bit.

'Do you write films?' he finally said.

'Umm . . . no, I work in advertising. Actually, uhh, never mind. What else? Are you still flying planes?' I stuttered.

'Yes. I was. But international travel will be on hold for some time. So I am here for a couple of months.'

'I know. I read it in the news,' I said as I bit the corner of my lip. I was so self-conscious that the words coming out of my mouth were irrational thoughts that hadn't become well-formed statements.

'That I am coming home?' he asked with a teasing grin.

I froze. 'No, that international travel will be on hold.' The words came out stilted, like a news reporter's.

Then I made no attempt at conversation. Nor did he. He must have felt awkward too.

'Take care,' he finally said and took off on his run.

'You too,' I whispered.

What a relief! Let me tell you, confronting your ex-boyfriend is trickier than they make it look in the movies. Even though I was seeing him after years, my blood almost froze. I don't know about him, but I stalked him intermittently on the internet until sometime ago. I stopped doing that when I learnt he was in love with someone else.

Suddenly, it started to rain heavily again. Wasn't it supposed to be sunny in March? The weather in the hills changes in the blink of an eye.

'Verona,' I shouted as I had almost lost Corona. I walked him back to the cottage. On reaching home, I went upstairs. Confused. Agitated. Unsettled.

Do you like to live in the present, diary? Of late, I have read many self-help books and most of them advise the reader, or listener, to live in the present. But in places like this, where there is no present, there is no option but to dive back into the past.

Meeting Nishit after so long sparked something in me. That spark also made me realize that I wrote about major parts of our doomed love story in my old diaries. I might get an idea for my movie script there. I went to the outhouse, Uncle Nick's library, and took out the old box where I had hidden most of my old diaries. Yes, thank God—they were still in the safe spot I had left them in.

I took them out, a deluge of them, starting from 2002. It was only recently that I had stopped maintaining a journal.

So, which one should I pick, diary? When did I last meet Nishit?

I guess it was in 2016. The worst year of my life. The worst days of my life.

See you soon,

Iti

The Red Muffler

22 March 2016

Dear Diary,

Today was the worst day of my life.

It would be untrue to say that I do not miss Nishit. It would be untrue to say that I have felt the same for any other boy before. It would be untrue to say that we decided to part ways because we fell out of love. It would be untrue to say that whenever I see an aircraft flying through the distant sky I don't wonder if Nishit is flying it!

Maybe Nishit will move on. Maybe, if we meet many years from now, it would be a good idea to expect a new beginning from a long-forgotten past. Then again, maybe it wouldn't be.

We officially met for the last time today. I can't hold back my tears as I pen my thoughts, pour them out to you. He will soon be leaving for Pune to pursue his commercial pilot training.

I will be moving to Delhi next month to pursue a degree in mass communication. St Mary's is the best college in Delhi University. That's the only reason I have to find happiness currently.

Our dreams fly high independently, but they don't work well together. If we never meet again, why not make our last meeting memorable?

Also, something really scary happened today. The moment he was about to sneak into my bedroom, Dad knocked on my door.

'I have bought a Pink Floyd limited edition for you,' he said through the door.

You know I don't have a smartphone yet. They will buy me my first one when I'm in Delhi. Monu uncle's shop deals in mobile phones. So I rushed to the balcony to hang a red muffler on the railing. Nishit would know that it's not safe to enter. Nishit and I have our own code language.

Then I opened the door to find Dad holding a big cardboard box wrapped in flashy paper. His aesthetic sense is probably the worst in the world. He's the kind who can't even put cello tape straight. When he wrapped my books with brown paper for school my friends and teachers would instantly know that I had taken help. But I love him. I can't imagine my life without him.

'Looks like a TV. How can a record be so huge?'

'It is your favourite. Pink Floyd limited edition. I requested Uncle Sam to send it from the US. This is your parting gift,' he said.

My dad can go to any lengths to see me smile. I swallowed the huge lump in my throat. After spending so many years in this house, it was time to leave. Be independent. Start on my own. Life is so strange; it changes beyond belief. I hugged him tighter than ever.

Have you ever moved out of your hometown to start a new life in the city? No, how could you? You're a non-living entity, my diary. But living things have to go through all this!

I have been the pampered kid. How will I live on my own, diary? The very thought of leaving my home and going to college fills me with anxiety. Have you ever found yourself shivering on a sleepless night because you can't imagine living on your own, diary?

No, of course not. You are dead, my diary.

'What are you thinking about?' Dad asked.

'Nothing,' I let out a sigh.

'Open it, kiddo,' he exclaimed.

'When am I getting my first phone?' I asked him again.

'In Delhi. I have already promised you,' he said, furrowing his eyebrows. He was trying to act as if he was annoyed but he really wasn't.

I unwrapped almost ten boxes, packed one inside the other, until I got my hands on the limited edition record. Dad tries to be super smart sometimes, but he fails miserably. What's the thrill of opening ten boxes when you already know what's inside the last one, diary? He doesn't even know how to plan a real surprise. But I did not say this to him. He might have felt bad, you know. He had put in so much effort to make me feel happy.

'Go ahead, play it,' he interrupted my lustful gaze from taking in every inch of the beautiful cover.

I had longed for this for so long.

Then, I played the record on my grandmother's old record player. My stomach leapt, ecstatic.

Their music is beyond this world, diary.

'Daddy, I don't want to go,' I said as 'Wish You Were Here' played in the background. I called him 'daddy' whenever I made impractical demands. I would act cute, like a pup who wants a good meal.

'In our universe, change is the only constant. If you try to structure the randomness of life, you're going against the law of nature,' he said, his voice level. He loves me but he knows no means to communicate this to me. He chooses science as his guard when he can't process his emotions.

'It's getting late, Dad! I have to go see off Nishit at the railway station tomorrow,' I reminded him.

'When are we supposed to leave?' he asked as he looked at his watch.

'At 5.45 sharp. His train leaves at 6.30 a.m.'

'Oh yes! I will be there. Sleep tight.' He kissed my forehead and left.

When Nishit entered my bedroom, the song had changed to 'High Hopes'.

'Will you miss me?' he asked me, sitting on the other side of my bed.

'Yes I will. Will you?'

When we don't have an answer, asking a counter-question is the most comfortable thing to do.

'Not always. Just when Pink Floyd plays,' he smiled.

For the last couple of months, ever since we had realized that farewell is a part of life, we run out of words on many occasions. A strange silence engulfed my room. Songs played, very low, one after the other. We held each other's hands and lay side by side until 4 a.m. Neither one of us slept that night. Time slipped by too fast, yet it felt like an eternity.

At one point, he leaned in to kiss me, but I pushed him away. Holding hands, at the most hugging each other, is the only physical thing we're allowed to do in our unsaid relationship pact.

I now regret it. I should have at least kissed him once. Now I might never know what kissing him feels like.

'You must speak to Shelly. It's time to make amends with her and move on. It was just a mistake. You can't be so stubborn,' he insisted before leaving.

'I'll try.' I could not promise him more than that. After what Shelly had done to me, it was hard to forget and forgive.

Deep wounds take time to heal, diary.

'I will call you on your new phone,' he promised.

'Don't promise me anything. You might find someone at the academy. Someone better than me,' I said. I was already insecure about his loyalty and commitment. I knew he would not be able to cope with the challenges of a long-distance relationship.

'You won't call me?' He looked at me anxiously, one eyebrow raised.

'I might also start seeing another guy at college,' I giggled.

'Why don't you feel we can be in a long-distance relationship?' His expression had not changed.

'Because it will never work. Sooner or later, one of us will move on,' I reaffirmed.

'I don't want to end it,' he insisted.

'I don't want to end it at a time when our differences become irreconcilable. If we end it on a good note, God knows, if we ever cross paths again, we might be together.'

'Where will our paths cross?'

'What's that place you dream of flying to? The one you were referring to on the terrace? The one you can't stop telling stories about since we were kids? Where the sun never sets?' I asked.

'Northern Norway!' he recollected.

'Hopefully there!'

'Promise me something?' Nishit held out his hand.

'Yes!' I said as I held his hand.

'You will write a book someday? Or a movie?' he asked with a hopeful smile.

'Why does it matter to you?' I asked.

'It matters to me because I love you. It matters to me because I want you to realize all your dreams.' He smiled. After all, it's our dreams, our career paths, that are steering us in different directions.

'You fly the planes. I will try,' I said.

'You must title your first movie *Where the Sun Never Sets*,' he said with unwavering belief in his voice.

'Why?' I quipped.

'That's the place that unites us, that's the place that divides us.' It is inexplicable how he can read the words in my mind.

'What does that mean?' I insisted he explain although I knew. I wanted to remember the words in his voice. It would be my happy memory of him if we never met again.

'It unites us forever, in our memories. And it divides us because it also represents our dreams. You want to be a movie scriptwriter and I want to be a pilot. So when I reach the place where the sun never sets, and you release your first film, it will be a gentle reminder that wherever we are, we are inseparable. We are soulmates,' he recited like a poem. A poem I will never forget.

'Nishit. Did you smoke up on the way here?' I said. I absorbed his words like a sponge absorbs water.

'The thought did cross my mind in the morning,' he replied.

'Nishit. You understand physics, philosophy and metaphysics. I have no clue what you've said! Please let us talk like normal human beings until you leave.' I let out a short laugh. Nishit was always my dad's favourite because he knew so much about science and the galaxy.

'Your dad didn't teach you enough science. Poor Mr Scientist. His daughter doesn't even understand a few fascinating concepts, which, by the way, if she does, will help her in her writing pursuit,' he said.

'Please leave,' I shouted. 'Not a word against my dad.'

'You're a dumbhead. That wasn't against your dad but you!' He kissed me on my forehead and left.

Dad came to wake me exactly on time as he had promised. I pretended to be fast asleep as I wept into my blanket. I have never cried so much in my life.

'Sayonara,' were the last words we uttered to each other at the Dehradun railway station.

Why can't your first relationship be your last, diary? Why do we have to endure so much pain in life, diary?

Dad's words reverberated in my mind: In our universe, change is the only constant. If you try to structure the randomness of life, you're going against the law of nature.

Riti Didi has also left for the US. You know, it's almost 12,000 km away from India. Who will I share my secrets with now, diary?

I can't tell Jay everything about my crushes; he is my little brother after all.

Will I be able to make friends in Delhi, diary?

Today is the worst day of my life. Don't feel like even writing anymore.

Sayonara!

Iti

The Green Muffler

23 March 2020

Dear Diary,

Today was a very confusing day, to be honest.

Covid-19 is finally here. But rather than washing my hands for ten minutes with soap and water, the first thing I did was to hang a green muffler on the balcony outside my room. I thought that if Nishit chose to pass by the house and still remembered our sign language he would drop by, preferably at night.

Should I remove the muffler, diary? Is it a childish thing to do, diary? I did think about it more than once. And he has not dropped by yet.

But I did confront Shyamala Aunty during breakfast. She was mean to me last night and interrupted my music session. I reminded her that she used to be my dad's aide in helping him gift me albums by my favourite artists. I also told her that I was playing none other than my favourite Pink Floyd. I played the record dad had gifted me all night.

How can she now be frustrated about me playing loud music, diary?

She pondered over this and finally decided to patch up with me. We are on good terms now.

Guess what happened next? The impossible. The arrogant Riti called us up. After years of not getting a call from her and receiving only a WhatsApp text from her even on Diwali, she just rang me up.

She introduced Shyamala Aunty and me to her current boyfriend Patrick. Shyamala Aunty freaked out when she found out that Riti has been living with him for more than a year now. She is planning her wedding this year. She has turned into a psycho.

'Meet Patrick,' she grabbed him by his collar and dragged him in front of the video camera. 'Say hello,' she instructed him as if he were a ten-year-old.

'Namaste!' Patrick said in a ridiculous accent. I couldn't stop laughing. But I could see that Shyamala Aunty was freaked out. Shyamala Aunty has taken care of us like her own children since we were little kids so she was full of motherly affection on seeing Riti.

'Hello, beta!' That's all she said before exiting the call. She dared not stay longer because Riti Didi isn't very fond of Shyamala Aunty. Had she stayed any longer she would have fallen prey to her cuss words.

On the other hand, I was forced to make conversation. 'How's the weather in Chicago?'

'It's windy here, mostly chilly,' Patrick replied. 'Fall is a good time to be here. Why don't you guys join us during Thanksgiving?'

'Covid-19 has been declared a pandemic. You guys should not move out. You guys must visit India if things are better by the end of this year. Perhaps during Diwali,' I said.

'Sure,' he said and exited the call.

'Every time you call me, Riti, I am nervous about what you will say next. The last time you called you were seeing a guy thrice your age. Are you serious about getting married to Patrick? What does he do for a living?' I asked her as if I were her elder sister.

'He has a band. He does not have a day job. But that's not a problem. I make way too much money. I can support three Patricks!' She let out a loud laugh. 'Isn't he hot?' she added.

'Iti, talk some sense into her,' Shyamala Aunty instructed me from a distance through weird hand gestures.

'Riti! Riti! Riti! You've turned out to be such a mess,' I said. 'Don't you ever feel like visiting me?' I asked her, straight to her face.

'Don't be jealous of me. Get yourself a decent guy. Goodbye.' That's all she said and hung up before I could even say bye to her.

She was not always like this. She left to pursue a master's degree five years ago. She promised to return on many occasions, but she never did. She gave us all possible excuses, from visa issues to college workload. Then she started working. She didn't come to India even once. Not even when Mom and Dad passed away.

With the global lockdown, it's almost stupid to expect her return. Maybe I'll have to forget and forgive.

I have become somebody who can't relate to getting married at Riti's age. Late twenties, I believe that is the right age to find a partner and settle down!

But playing video games is justified at almost any age. So that day, I played my new favourite video game all through the afternoon. I didn't write a single word. I tried starting the script but could not think of something super cool. So I dropped the idea. I am now venturing into things that I have never done before. Maybe trying out new things will unblock my mind. It's a creative process, I should not force ideas. I still have time before the lockdown is lifted.

Later in the evening, I planted a rose. Shyamala Aunty taught me grafting. She said, 'It is as simple as cutting one of the main branches of a plant and sowing it in a new pot.

'If you water it every day, it will eventually grow roots and we can plant it as a new plant here.'

'I feel like I am a newly planted rose waiting for my roots to grow in my new surroundings,' I replied.

While it is my own garden, I haven't been back since my parents passed away.

The last memories I have of this house are full of painful events. This lockdown will give me a chance to register new feelings and happy memories.

'Riti hasn't changed a bit,' Shyamala Aunty said.

'Oh yes!' I replied.

'One day she will find her way back home. One day everyone has to find their way back home,' she said with a smile.

'She won't come back. She never cared about the family. She never cared about anyone. She was the most selfish kid. Dad knew it, always,' I said to emphasize that her conviction may be unfounded. Not every bird finds its way back home. Some birds are lost forever on the journey of migration they make every winter. Maybe Riti Didi is one of those lost birds.

'She will come back. I know it in my heart,' Shyamala Aunty said again.

'Oh my God! Shyamala Aunty, why don't you realize that she won't? What is wrong with you?' I yelled.

Deep within I just want Riti Didi back in my life. But whenever reality hits me hard, and I am faced with the truth that she won't come back, it becomes very painful.

'She hasn't found closure yet. Running away from your problems can only take you so far. One day you have to face them and overcome them,' Shyamala Aunty reaffirmed with confidence.

'What do you mean?' I asked her, baffled.

'You are no different, Iti. You've been running from this home since your parents passed away. You never came back either. Had it not been for the lockdown, you would not have come back. Your sister is running just like you were,' she said calmly.

'But I did come back once from hostel after I received the news. I attended the funeral. The last rites were performed right in front of me,' I said as tears rolled down my cheeks. I had shed enough tears to fill up a bucket.

Shyamala Aunty hugged me as she said, 'You are brave, beta. You were always the bravest. You found your closure.'

'There isn't a single day when I don't think about them. How have I found my closure? I haven't. Jay hadn't even seen college. What did my poor little brother do to deserve such a hard fate?' I said helplessly.

'Life is not always in our control. Therefore, we have faith in God,' she said.

Shonu-Monu came along asking for dinner and so Shyamala Aunty had to leave. I spent almost an hour alone thinking about the people that once used to be a part of my life in Mussoorie. Days when this little world of mine meant the world to me. Days when love ruled over aspirations. Days when I wasn't so lonely that I did not have anyone to talk to let alone call.

As I looked at the sky change colour from orange to deep red, I realized that I couldn't help but wonder where Shelly was, diary. What would she be doing now, diary?

I had lied to Nishit that night when we met. I was reminded of my lie when I read my old diary last night. I didn't even try to get back in touch with her after that incident happened. I did look for her on Facebook two years ago after getting sloshed. But I could not find her. Would she have returned to Mussoorie before the lockdown just like the rest of us, diary?

I don't have anything else to share for now. Let me get back to reading my old diaries. Maybe they hold some clue to Shelly's current whereabouts. Maybe I should make amends as a grown-up now and reach out to her.

The only words I penned today were: You are not guilty about someone else progressing, you are guilty about not moving enough. Set individual goals and achieve them. When you look up to someone, don't feel jealous. Look up to them and feel inspired.

Ta-ta,

Iti

The Dance

24 December 2012

Dear Diary,

Today was the best day of my life.

My best friend Shelly and I danced on stage in front of the entire school. We performed a salsa to 'Rhythm Divine' followed by a meringue to 'Un Dos Tres'. It was the school's annual function.

Varun Sir, our dance teacher, is very happy. He might throw us a success party at the newly inaugurated café, Himalayan Treasures, in Landour. I will soon get a chance to escape somewhere with Shelly without parental supervision. How cool is that, diary?

I have been very busy with dress rehearsals and green room gossip lately. I have not had the chance to write in my diary for weeks. So much has happened. So much is about to happen.

I think I am in love. Sometimes, I eat a lot. Sometimes, I am so excited I hardly feel like eating. I dance in the shower. I sing on the school bus. Being in love is like chasing those playful butterflies you can never catch. How can you? They're in your stomach.

You know how hard it is to get a position on stage, but we nailed it with our talent and hard work. Chaudhary Ma'am had written the classic saying 'Slow and steady wins the race' on the blackboard in our corridor as the thought for the day. I second her.

Shelly and I are officially the best dancers in our school now.

Mom and Dad heaped praise on me. Shelly's parents also attended the function. But that is not exactly why today was the best day. Something happened. Something that has never happened before. Guess?

Shelly gave me a big surprise. She spoke with our senior Abhay's friend and arranged for a meeting with Abhay after we got off the stage. He was smiling and waiting for us in the green room. His smile was as beautiful as the sky during the sunset.

'You guys rocked the stage,' he said as he shook Shelly's hand.

'Thank you,' she said. 'Meet my partner-in-crime, Iti. She is a huge fan of your captaincy.' Abhay was the captain of my house.

My blood froze. I could not speak a word. Nor could I move my hand to shake his. The three of us kept looking at each other in awkward silence. I kept looking at Abhay without blinking. He is the most handsome guy on earth. Whenever I look at him, my reaction is the same. I have been following him around the school campus. I can't share this with many people. They all think I am a good girl. And you know, good girls are only supposed to get high grades and do extra-curricular activities. Good girls are not supposed to have crushes and follow boys. I want to maintain my reputation as a good girl in school. I am very conscious about what people think of me, you know that.

Finally, I moved my stone-cold hand forward and shook his as I said, 'Hi!' in a meek tone.

The moment he held my hand, a jolt of electricity flowed through my body. It was stronger than the kind Professor Jain talks about in science lectures. I wanted to hold him and kiss him like I had imagined a million times in my dreams. He is my first crush, you know that. I had never been so close to him before. The closest was when I caught a glimpse of him drinking water from the water cooler on our floor. Since he is two years my senior, his classroom is on the floor above ours. Juniors are not allowed on that floor.

Riti Didi tells me about her crushes all the time. But this is the first time I have felt something of this sort.

Shelly and I are in the same house, so we get to spend the extra periods together. Now, all we do is discuss Abhay. Shelly hasn't had a crush yet. She mostly listens to me. I just hope she will hold my secret as you do.

We are the star dancers of our house now. Will it impress Abhay? Tell me, diary. Tell me! Sometimes, it's so frustrating that you don't talk. I feel so much at ease with you. You're better than our school counsellor Rita Ma'am. Rita Ma'am only talks about sex education these days. That's her favourite topic since our senior Amisha got pregnant. Mohit's backbencher gang shames her every day. Nobody judges the guy Keyur, who got her pregnant.

Why is the world so anti-women, diary?

Talking of school, I still remember the summer day when I first saw Abhay. Our house is called 'Buddha House' or 'Green House'. Abhay was being honoured with the badge of captaincy along with Madhusmita. While Shelly instantly became a fan of Madhusmita, I was attracted to Abhay.

He turned my life upside down in the months that followed. Now, everything I do, I do to get his attention. All I want is to be with him. I take part in more intra-school competitions, keep my hair tidy and shave my legs often.

Shelly knows this well. I tell Shelly about everything in my life. She's the friend God blesses only the lucky ones with. God knows what I have done to have her support in my life.

It is time to sleep. It is time to dream. It is time to be in that one place where Abhay and I are inseparable. We just can't stop cuddling. Don't tell anyone. Sometimes I do want to go beyond cuddling. Shelly got us a blue film DVD last week. I know it's the worst of people who watch blue films, but they are being traded like commodities in stock markets on our campus. I was just curious. I swear to God that I will never indulge in such a sinful act ever. I haven't mustered the courage to watch it yet. But someday, I will. Possibly when I am closer to becoming an adult. That is what I keep reminding Shelly as well. But she has more exposure than I do. Especially because most of her cousins live in the West. She comes from a family with quite a modern outlook.

I imagine that when I grow up I will work very hard and build an amazing career. Maybe then Abhay will be attracted to me. I feel I am not as good-looking as he is, so there is no way he would want to have a romantic relationship with me. But once I am successful, I will make him meet Mom and Dad. If everything goes as per the plan, we will get married in 2020. I will be twenty-two years old then. That should be an ideal age to get married.

I also have to tell you everything that happened to Riti Didi tomorrow. She is my favourite. She's more than a sister. She is my best pal and confidant.

Although she is more concerned about sharing her stories, I can share some of my secrets with her. Since we trade secrets in return for secrets we have a pact that neither one of us will leak anything to our parents. It is our sibling deal.

I am feeling very sleepy now. Good night!

Buh-byeee,

Iti

The Yellow Pages

14 February 2013

Dear Diary,

This week has been the roughest week of my life.

'I want to slice him like a knife slices bread. I want to dissolve in him like the chocolate that finds solace in milk. Yet I am unsure whether he feels the same,' Shelly read out loud from you, my diary.

I was scared for a moment as Mom and Dad were downstairs. What if they read the kind of thoughts I am having these days? Oh my God. Even the mere thought of it makes me want to puke. You, my diary, hold some of my very private thoughts.

Yes, I have made Shelly read some lines from you. But I never gave her permission to open you and start reading. She gets playful at times, you know.

'You can write erotica,' she said, continuing to tease me. I kept mum. But I had made up my mind to find a box soon and hide you in it in my uncle's outhouse. I wasn't as scared about her reading my words as I was about my parents reading them.

'Leave it,' I told her as I snatched you from her hands and placed you under the bed.

What had happened two days ago at school was enough to scare me. Diary, I am so grateful to have Shelly in my life.

Rekha Ma'am, our social science teacher, had asked us to bring in the notebooks in which we were supposed to write about the French Revolution. She asks us to write out most of the things from our textbook as she believes writing and speaking out loud while writing will help us remember important dates and facts.

Little does she know that history as a subject sucks, and no matter how much we write, it's impossible to remember all the dates.

But anyway, that's not important. I have this stupid habit of beating around the bush.

I had accidentally submitted you along with my notebook. Thankfully, the diary doesn't mention whom it belongs to, and Shelly had not submitted her notebook that day.

The next day Rekha Ma'am entered the class and distributed everyone's notebooks. But she also mentioned getting her hands on a diary that she shouldn't have received. She asked the owner to go to the staff room and collect it from her in person.

I almost fainted.

Shelly and I sit on the same bench. She sometimes senses things even without being told about them. She's the most understanding person I know. I am so lucky to have her in my life.

She told me not to worry and that we would figure it out together. I did not speak a word for the rest of that day. I did not even have lunch and was scolded by Mom for not eating my tiffin. You know how furious Mom gets when she finds out that I have not been eating well!

But miraculously, that night, Shelly came to my place. And guess what, she had rescued my diary just like PETA rescues puppies.

My happiness knew no bounds. Her dad is an influential guy in our town, the rich dad, you know. I had assumed she had managed to get my diary using her family's power.

I did not even bother to ask her. How silly am I, diary?

Nishit, who is working with me on a science project, later told me that she'd lied to the teacher that the diary belonged to her and faced the punishment of writing out the lesson ten times. Nishit and Shelly know each other as they also happen to be family friends.

I sometimes feel Nishit makes an extra effort to speak to me, but how do I tell him that I am head over heels in love with our senior Abhay? I will tell Shelly to tell him one day.

Had Nishit never told me what Shelly had done, I would've never known. I do owe him a treat for that. He made me realize how lucky I am to have Shelly in my life.

You know why I am telling you about Nishit today?

It's because I want to share about him. And I can't tell Shelly everything I feel as she might tell him, given that they've known each other since childhood.

But the other day when I was entering class, I was bullied by the famous Mohit's backbencher gang. They're a bunch of business-class assholes who were born with a silver spoon and just come to school to pass their time. They've got no interest in studying and no ambition to become anything.

Shelly wants to pursue fashion and I want to become a successful doctor. I also want to become a writer, but I am convinced that becoming a doctor is a good choice for my financial life.

Am I right in thinking so, my dear diary?

Mom and Dad think that becoming a doctor is better than wanting to pursue mass communication. However, my dad's first choice is anything to do with mathematics or physics. But I am not made for that. I know that I have to put in twice as much effort as Nishit for our science project.

Oh God! I forgot to tell you about Nishit again.

So, Mohit's infamous gang started calling me Ghonsla like on any other day. I ignored them like on any other day and entered the classroom.

Initially, when they would loudly address me as Ghonsla, I used to get nervous and my body would shake as I made my way to my seat. Shelly taught me to face those rascals with confidence and pay no heed to their presence.

But on that day, this classmate of mine, Nishit, was there and he walked up to Mohit and asked him not to hurl abuse at students. Mohit got so agitated that most of the guys from our class had to rush to calm them down before their war of words went down in history as World War III.

While the war induced by elevated levels of testosterone could be averted, the one induced by elevated levels of oestrogen in my home somehow couldn't be averted. That is because when I got back home, I couldn't stop myself from fighting with Mom. Dad had to intervene like a firefighter equipped to calm the volcanoes!

Mom has somehow become the biggest vamp of my life. 'It was your idea to cut my beautiful long hair into a short bob that looks like a bird's nest,' I shouted at her.

Given that I also wear thick glasses and have braces, I am exactly the kind of nerd who is bullied wherever they go. I had such pretty, long hair. It was becoming a daunting task for Shyamala Aunty to oil and braid it regularly before school.

How could Abhay ever be in love with me now, diary?

If New York has the Statue of Liberty, Mussoorie has the Statue of Hilarity. And yeah, that's me!

But it kind of felt good that Nishit took my side. I also feel that he is a very good boy.

'I'm sorry,' Shelly said as she broke my reverie.

'Is the letter ready?' she asked.

'What?'

'The proposal letter you are supposed to write for Abhay,' she reminded me.

'Oh no!' I acted as if I had completely forgotten about it, but I knew what she was referring to.

'Pick up a pen and paper and start without further delay,' Shelly insisted.

'I don't think it's a good idea!' I tried to convince her.

'I told you the same thing. But you told me that it is easier for you to express your feelings on paper. I had always insisted on the phone call,' Shelly rebuked me.

'I definitely can't telephone him. Besides, we don't have his phone number.'

'You are a dumbhead, we can search for it in the yellow pages,' she told me.

'No we can't,' I said reluctantly.

'Yes we can. Do you know his school bus number?'

And that's the problem with living in a small town. It is a small world where anything and everything can be figured out!

'Yes, it's thirteen, the devil's number,' I murmured.

'I can find out his phone number then,' she said as she ran downstairs to get the yellow pages, which are in the drawer of the telephone table. She knows everything about my home. It is kind of her home. She's been coming here for a long time.

'What's his surname?' she asked as she entered the room, already scanning through the yellow pages.

'Minhaz,' I said reluctantly.

'Bus thirteen goes down the hill, off the mall road. So his house has to be somewhere near Cliff Hall Estate on Cart Road. Let me check every surname in that area. Do you realize that we have gotten kind of lucky here?' She smiled as she ran her finger down every yellow page entry of Cart Road residents.

'How did we get lucky?' I asked her sceptically. I prayed to God that we did not find his phone number. I wasn't prepared to go through the arduous experience of calling him up with butterflies in my stomach and cold feet.

Then, as my bad luck would have it, somehow always has it, it seems to be the constant source of demotivation in my life, she found his phone number.

'Here it is,' she jumped in joy. I almost fell off the bed.

'No, no, no, no, no,' I said. 'This isn't happening.'

'You've got to have the courage to express your feelings out loud,' Shelly said. 'You can't hide behind the pages of your diary all through your life. Call him up and tell him. We either go north or south. We are not going to wait forever.'

'Why are you doing this to me?' I felt like crying because of the pressure she was putting on me.

'Because I care for you. I love you. Of course, as a friend though.' She smiled and placed a reassuring arm around my shoulder.

Suddenly, I got the courage to make a move.

I asked her to check if my parents were asleep so they wouldn't pick up the main telephone downstairs and overhear my conversation. I don't know why teenagers act crazy all the time.

She checked and assured me that everything was in order. She dialled the number. We had decided that if anyone else from his family picked up, we would keep mum and disconnect the call.

After three or four rings, the call was answered. We did not think it would be so quick. Gosh! My anxiety knew no bounds. Shelly put the phone on speaker as he uttered, 'Jannat, I was waiting for your call desperately. What took you so long?'

Shelly looked at me in disbelief. I looked at her as tears rolled down my cheeks. She disconnected the call without uttering a word.

But now I know that Abhay has a girlfriend, and she is none other than our volleyball team captain and the most crushed on senior, Jannat Khan. But they have kept it so low-key at school. It's probably because Jannat's twin brother Imran is their classmate too. Maybe she doesn't want it to get to her family.

I cried and cried and cried some more. I cried until my eyes dried up and I couldn't cry anymore.

Now, the sky looks pale, and that rainbow has shattered. That constant smile on my face has also faded away like the colour of Mussoorie in January when the snow covers it all.

Bye,
Pity on Iti

Movie Script Idea

26 March 2020

Dear Diary,

I am very happy today.

Finally, reading old diary entries has led me to some ideas for my movie script.

What is fiction, diary? They say fiction is a figment of one's imagination. But even figments of imagination have a small part of our real experiences. Is the truth stranger than fiction, diary? Or is fiction stranger than the truth?

No matter what one believes in, I know for sure that reel life is inspired by real life much more than real life is inspired by reel life.

Shyamala Aunty was correct. The best of stories have an element of real stories in them. With her advice, and some real-life beliefs of my own, I have started writing a thriller about a young woman named Smiti (you know it's me, Iti) who sneaks out every night during the lockdown with her pet dog Verona (I am using my dog's name as it is because he won't mind, unlike humans). I have made Shyamala Aunty a character called Vanita who is an accomplice of the protagonist Smiti and assists her during her nightly escapades. As the house helps know every story in the neighbourhood, Vanita helps Smiti discover some untold stories of her neighbourhood.

This is my script summary:

Amidst the worldwide lockdown, a young advertising copywriter, Smiti, moves back to her hometown upon being fired from her job. Smiti's house help, Vanita, makes her realize that this is an opportunity to work on her first-ever movie script. Smiti has always wanted to be a writer but worked in advertising to pay off her college loan.

However, it isn't easy to have a stream of ideas for a movie script flowing. After two days of endless surfing on the internet and exploring possible story ideas, she feels helpless about finishing this task.

As Smiti is faced with writer's block, Vanita offers to take her out every night while the city sleeps and helps her discover the best of stories from the neighbourhood in return for shelter in her garage.

Vanita takes her to a quarantine facility nearby where they meet a pregnant woman Olivia, an Italian tourist Lorenzo, and a student from an exchange programme Kylie, among others.

She later meets a charismatic pilot Nihaal (of course, he is inspired by Nishit) among other tourists. Smiti and Nihaal fall in love in these unprecedented times.

As the days pass, Vanita helps her see more than her posh neighbourhood, helps her discover the other side of town, and during the lockdown, Smiti explores the fragility of life and the extreme situations some people are facing due to the lockdown.

With almost no cash, just a few sets of clothing, and nothing to brag or show off about, Smiti and Vanita explore the three most important questions about life.

Who are you? Why are you here? What should you do?

As the days pass, and her story progresses, Smiti sees her best memories and worst nightmares come to life.

Will writing a story prove to be an adventure worth taking to battle being fired from her job? Will life be the same . . . ever?

Now, this is going to be the twist:

After she has written more than eighty per cent of her script, Vanita disappears. Smiti keeps roaming the streets in search of her but is unable to find her. Moreover, she was so engrossed in listening to Vanita's stories that she didn't pay attention to where the quarantine facility was located and is unable to find her way back there through the sinuous alleys that make up the neighbourhood on the other side of her posh locality.

She keeps waiting for Vanita to return but eventually gives up and writes the ending to the story. When the lockdown is lifted, Vanita appears and when Smiti asks her why she had suddenly disappeared, she tells Smiti that she was in her home through the lockdown and that Smiti was the first person she was visiting after the lockdown was lifted. Smiti faints only to realize that being isolated at home through the lockdown has affected her sanity.

The story has no closure. It is up to the viewers to decide whether Vanita is lying about not coming back before or if Vanita is a figment of Smiti's imagination, just like every other character in her story. The quarantine facility could also be a figment of her imagination, existing only in the articles Smiti read about Covid-19 on the internet.

You know what? Maybe, Nihaal and Smiti will meet in the end. That could be the happy ending that gives a sense of some closure to the viewers.

I have given my script a working title already: 'Where the Sun Never Sets'.

That's about it. I have scheduled a call with Kajol Sir. I hope he likes my script as much as I do!

I worked on it for almost three days. I was so busy that I could not spare the time to share my thoughts even with you. This thriller is going to be 'the best social thriller movie of 2020'.

I can already see myself winning awards. This is the most interesting part about me. I imagine so much that sometimes it's hard to draw a line between the real and the imaginary. But daydreaming helps me see dreams that I work hard to realize later.

My movie will talk about how difficult the lockdown was for people who were isolated and what repercussions it had on people's mental health. Everybody talks about the economic repercussions of the lockdown, but I want to highlight the mental health issues it caused.

I wish you could 'speak' my diary. I need you to boost my morale. I want you to hug me and tell me that I am an amazing storyteller. I want you to validate me. I lack someone who has that kind of complete trust in me.

Anyway, enough sharing for now. Good night. Let me get back to reading my old diaries for some kick-ass ideas that can be added to this script before I pitch it to Kajol Sir!

Godspeed,

Iti

Self-development

5 April 2020

Dear Diary,

Today was one of the most exciting-cum-nerve-racking days of my life.

This is how you feel when you appear for a job interview. After I had been working on my script for almost ten days, Kajol Sir finally set up a time for me to call him and share my progress. I was so excited to hear his thoughts.

Kajol Sir is keen on innovative stuff and has an eye for detail. When I worked on the famous prime-time advertisement *'Sahi hai'* for a top insurance company, he handheld me through the process. Our advertisement debuted during the Indian Premium League (IPL). We received uncountable selfie video entries for the contest from participants from all over India. That was the best project I delivered, and it was done within seven months of my joining W&W. Kajol Sir threw a success party for the team. He saw the potential in me and therefore has encouraged me to push myself a little harder every time.

But on the flip side, he gets critical at times as he wants me to improve my storytelling craft. However encouraging the latter part may sound, the truth is that I am always a little scared before presenting to him. He is my boss! Like I am your boss, dear diary. You have to patiently listen to everything that I have to say.

'Hello, Sir! How is the lockdown treating you?' I said in an attempt to get the conversation going smoothly while my hands and feet had frozen.

'Bored of washing my hands and changing masks,' he laughed as he added, 'None fit on top of my nose. It's annoying how they make my glasses fog up.'

'It's true, Sir.' I laughed. He likes it when people laugh at his unconventional comments.

'So what's new? Tell me the idea you're working on,' he came straight to the point without beating around the bush.

So I told him all about my idea. He listened until the very end. He did not say a word in between. I felt as at ease sharing my ideas with him as I do with you, my diary.

So? You must be wondering what happened. Did the idea go through smoothly?

The answer is no.

He explained to me, ‘While the story is very interesting, it won’t appeal to the Indian audiences. Indian audiences like emotional, feel-good stories. They don’t care about the thrill. And we aren’t Netflix to come up with the best content, are we?’

He added, ‘People focus on unimportant things every day to lose focus on the bigger things in life. It helps distract them from the more important questions in life. Our job is to entertain them with a story that keeps them distracted. Why do you want them to focus on the important questions about life like who are you? Why are you here? What should you do?’

‘Uh huh . . . ’ I listened to him like a kid who gets beaten up in the park by friends for coming to the park and again gets beaten up by the family for going to the park, while all she ever wanted was some moments of joy as she played.

‘Mental health issues? Nobody cares about this in India. Talk about the financial and economic crisis, please.’

I had no answer to that. As a writer, I knew I would get carried away and not analyse the market potential of the story. I would just think about how good the story was because I felt the same.

Then, he went on to explain, ‘We have to reach the masses, not the urban audiences. Your story will connect with the urban audience only.’

When I could not say a word because I had gone into shock, wondering how to come up with the next idea, he continued, 'You're a first-time scriptwriter. A thriller is for mature writers. I am not sure you'll be able to tie up the loose ends and come up with a fine story.' As he spoke I kept rotating the ring on my middle finger.

Now, that's where my confidence broke. I am not sure how I will come up with a feel-good drama. I thought for a while that I would write about my family's story. The only happening and devastating 'drama' of my life. But, I will not enjoy writing about it. It will force me to walk down memory lane and feel every moment. I am not sure that I am ready to face every event from my past right now.

I wish I could write sci-fi for Hollywood. But Nishit and Dad felt I wouldn't be able to do that due to my limited knowledge of physics and the universe. I felt like going back in time and telling them to shut up because the market doesn't care about such complicated concepts. They want a feel-good emotional story.

I spent the rest of the day practising yoga and mindfulness. I am very stressed out these days. Not being able to move out of the house has taken a toll on my mental health, so I decided to go out wearing a mask in the name of buying groceries. I did not buy a thing though. I'm blessed to have Shyamala Aunty in my life. She takes care of everything.

I sneaked into an antique shop in Landour, that also served as a home and was therefore open during the lockdown, while strolling on the streets, and bought a telescope from 1920. It did cross my mind that I could get a better deal online, but I finally bought it from the local shop because I realized 2020 would not be the best year for local businesses.

I spent the evening landscape-gazing, discovering some beautiful Garhwali homes and temples in the faraway blue mountains, some birds here and there, and now I'm waiting for the midnight sky full of stars to shine in all its glory.

Sometimes the mountains call me back to lay in their embrace and feel the sunshine. To become free of all attachments back in the city; to gaze through the canopy of pine trees into the endless blue sky; to feel every second become an hour as one never runs out of time in the mountains; to breathe, eat and drink pure air, food and water; to see the stars melt in front of my eyes faster than snow; to play with furry dogs and cats; to listen to the divine music of rustling trees and sometimes to listen to absolutely nothing for hours. A trip to the mountains is a journey to the self, and therefore, to God.

As I pondered through the sunset I realized that the only way 2021 could be a better year for everyone was if each one of us became kind enough to support local communities, businesses and people. A beautiful year can only be promised if we start thinking beyond ourselves. The next time you decide to buy, also ask yourself the question—how will it impact the local community? How can you be a change agent for the people whose lives were impacted in 2020?

Maybe I should write something on similar lines. Maybe Kajol Sir wants me to think on similar lines.

Leave-taking,

Iti

Forever

6 April 2020

Dear Diary,

It was a lovely day today!

The lockdown was partially lifted for a day. What a relief.

'We can go out to buy essentials. We have to wear masks and practise social distancing,' Shyamala Aunty kept yelling and repeating these words. She was paranoid that whoever went out today would come back home with the virus. As if they were selling viruses and not groceries in the store.

'It is advisable that the younger ones step out as the virus is dangerous for older people, especially those like me with a blood pressure problem,' she said. She has figured out from WhatsApp University that she's in the high-risk zone for developing complications from the infection. I don't want her to live in the fear of contracting the virus and therefore I have volunteered to go out as and when need be. It allows me to come back home with new ideas.

'Chill! I will take care. I am a grown-up now. Yes, I will follow all the protocols. I love you and would never do anything that would pose a threat to your life. So please calm down,' I reassured her.

Shyamala Aunty doesn't know about my solo escapades around Mussoorie. I wake up every day at the same time and leave home in the hope of finding Nishit in the park. I sneak out so Shyamala Aunty doesn't know that I am going out. Unfortunately, I have not run into him. He must not be moving out, though his younger brother, who probably has little regard for the lockdown, might be. Pity, I want to know what is going on in Nishit's life. Of course, I also have the selfish motive of getting some stories out of him. His life must be full of adventures, travel and sports.

What if he is still single and wants to get back together with me, diary? I am a hopeless person, you know, my diary. I won't change so soon.

I know him well. Or, to be more precise, I knew him well.

You know, diary, India has the highest population of young people in the world. Going by that, even if some of us die, it wouldn't be a major loss to the economy. We would be martyred for our older counterparts. The funny part is, shouldn't we be protecting the young? But the masses are emotional. People are not practical! That's what Kajol Sir was trying to explain to me the other day. I need to start on an emotional story soon.

As for today, I went to Sanskriti Super Mart. Most of the people in our area prefer to visit this store as it is a one-stop-shop.

'Get at least thirty tetra packs of milk,' Shyamala Aunty shouted as I kickstarted my scooter. The first thing I observed on reaching Sanskriti was the big blackboard that showcased deals of the day. 'Milk Out of Stock' was written on it in bold letters.

Life is unpredictable. More so in the times of Covid.

I picked up the rest of the stuff and then went to The Gourmet Shop. This is where the uber-rich shop, not the middle-class families, the guy who directed me towards the store had carefully pointed out. But 'milk' was all Shyamala Aunty ever needed so I had no option but to make a detour to the store on my way back home.

I stood in line, six feet apart from the man in front of me, who was scared to death by the sneezing woman six feet behind me, for ten minutes. This line moved faster than the one in Sanskriti, and I felt less panicked here. These folks must be maintaining the needed hygiene. The rich can't be physically malnourished so instead, they acquire obsessive compulsive disorder (OCD), mental malnourishment. First World problems, dear diary!

The security guard checked our body temperature. We were also advised to sanitize our hands before entering both the shops. The 'new normal' was scary. All through our lives we have lived in groups, eaten lunch in groups, watched movies in groups, organized parties in groups. Suddenly, being close to other people, without actually being close, scared the shit out of me.

'Please stand aside, Ma'am,' the guard told me and left. Oh God! I knew these protocols could turn out to be a major problem for me. My body temperature is always a degree above normal. It's how I am made, and I can't change it.

Then, the most bizarre thing happened.

The security guard came back with Shelly. I knew it was her behind the mask. I recognize every bit of her personality, the way she talks, moves, sits, walks.

'What's the matter?' her tone was brisk.

'Her temperature is a degree above normal but not high enough to count as fever. Should I let her in?' the guard asked.

'Yes,' she said and started walking back towards a little cabin beside the billing counters.

'Hey! Wait. It's me, Iti,' I said.

'I know. Follow me.' She kept walking without bothering to turn around to reply.

She pulled up a chair for me and then sat on the other side of the table. Her cosy cabin was beautiful. It overlooked the Dhauladhar Range of the Himalayas. It looked as if a photoshopped poster was pasted across the French windows. The look and feel of the shop was straight out of a Parisian movie from the 1950s.

'How are you, Shelly? Where have you been all these years?'

'I'm good. I'm married to the store owner. I am looking after the store part-time as there is nothing much to do during the lockdown. In-laws, you know? Can't spend the whole day at home,' she replied.

'You got married? Are you not pursuing fashion?'

'I pursued my bachelors in fashion as I had always wanted. I own a boutique in Singapore. My husband helped me set up the business,' she replied calmly.

'I hope you're not upset with me after what happened.' No. I did not mean to be so straight. But the words came out of my mouth like chips that fall across the floor when you tear the packet in haste.

'To be honest, I was very upset with you. I never wanted to see you again. But I guess I have moved on now. Will you have some masala chai?' She seemed unperturbed by my sudden recalling of the forgotten past.

'You do remember my love for chai,' I smiled.

'How can I ever forget,' she said with a hint of pain in her voice as she waved at a staff member. 'Get two masala chais. Sanitize the mugs!'

'Okay Ma'am,' the thin little boy nodded and left on her command.

'What are you up to these days?' she asked, breaking my frenzied examination of every corner of the shop. Her husband must be a top shot, I thought, the kind who runs many businesses and happens to have a family business back in their hometown to conceal the black money.

'I am working on a movie script,' I said rather slowly.

'Oh! Wow. That's your job?' She got excited for the first time. She wasn't as excited when she first saw me.

'No, unfortunately, it is not. I write jingles for ads. This is my first script. Our boss has asked us to work on something innovative given we don't have a lot of client revenue flowing in,' I replied.

'Hmm. What kind of ads?' she asked.

'Did you watch the *Sahi hai* series of the Life Insurance Company of India (LIC)?' I mentioned my most popular ad.

'No. I am mostly in Singapore. I am not a TV buff either,' she said in the accent most NRIs have on their return from a foreign country.

'Me neither,' I said as I felt despondent.

'It is your job!' She broke into laughter.

'To write. Not to watch,' I said with an eyebrow raised.

A poster with the words 'Hatred, jealousy and apathy come from insecurity. There is nothing wrong with the world. There is something wrong with you.

Fix it to make way for love and compassion and you will always respond from a place of security' hung on the wall behind her.

I kept absorbing details about the room until she said, 'So, what is this about?'

'Milk cartons. The Sanskriti store ran out. People are overstocking these days, you know,' I educated her as I presumed she might not be updated about the state of affairs in this country. She did have an air about returning from Singapore.

'No, the movie story,' she asked me exactly what I didn't want to speak to anyone about. You know, diary!

'Oh, the story. I don't know. I wrote a summary of one. But my boss did not approve it. I am still to finalize a new one,' I replied.

'Would you mind if I suggest an idea?' She rose from her chair in excitement.

'Oh, sure. Why not?' I am open to getting ideas from anywhere now.

'Write about the tough and testing times that we as humans have been put through. You could draw a parallel to something similar that happened in the past,' she said.

'In the past?' I asked hesitantly.

'Lockdown has happened for us as a generation for the first time. But some of our ancestors would have been through a pandemic. Or been in situations similar to a lockdown. British colonization would have felt similar to the inhabitants of the colonies in the past,' she affirmed.

'That's very interesting, Shelly. Thank you so much for the idea. Shyamala Aunty suggested something on similar lines as well.' I was dumbstruck to realize that everyone except for me was thinking on similar lines. Masses are emotional. Maybe Kajol Sir is right.

'Oh! Please don't mention it. I have these thoughts all the time. I am an avid reader, you know that. Maybe someday I will write a book. But currently, I am too lazy to pen my thoughts. I am glad to see someone execute ideas. You've always been the girl with her notes in the diary,' she chuckled.

I wanted to spend more time with her. She is the best and always has been. But I feared she would bring up the past. I don't want to walk down that path now. Somewhere deep down, because of the time that has passed, I think all is well between us. I got up and insisted that I couldn't stay for long as my paranoid caretaker was awaiting my return.

We can't expect people to be as they were when we last met them. Sometimes, they change for the better. Sometimes, for the worse. Shelly seemed to have learnt from her mistakes. Without having the tea, I left with the promise of seeing her again.

There's something I realized today, though. Friends like Shelly can only be made at a certain age. She was warm and welcoming and made sure that I had a comfortable experience. I miss this warmth that small towns have to offer when I'm in Gurgaon. Much to my happiness, her shop was playing songs from the 1990s. Vengaboys helped me reminisce about my childhood.

It was a lovely feeling being on my own while riding my scooter on the hills. Coincidentally, I was listening to the Vengaboys that morning.

I believe that every person I cross paths with has a unique story to share, and I have something to learn from them. I have never had a constant role model as no human being is perfect. But I do have so many good things to learn from every individual. Even the most negative of people have something to offer—they teach us not to be negative in life.

Are you irreplaceable in someone's life, diary?

Shelly was always irreplaceable in my life. But Dad was right. Change is the only constant.

I was wrong to have assumed when we got into the fight that she was wrong. Maybe, self-acceptance was the biggest fight for her. Maybe it still is.

Why would she marry a guy otherwise, diary?

In life, there are no absolute rights. There are no absolute wrongs. One has to choose right and wrong.

I came back home and went to the outhouse. It was time to read about everything we had gone through in the past. Maybe that will give me some additional ideas.

'What is the progress on the movie script?' Shyamala Aunty asked as she entered the outhouse.

'I am still trying to finalize the plot. Any help is appreciated. Not entering the room and disturbing my flow is also appreciated,' I rebuked her.

'Write about people you know. Things close to you. Everyone relates to such stories,' she advised.

'Thank you for your advice. Now I need to get some work done,' I asked Shyamala Aunty to leave and shut the door behind her.

Then, I began scribbling all over you again, my dear diary.

Ciao,

Iti

The Terrace—1

14 February 2014

Dear Diary,

Today was the most phenomenal day of my life.

The doorbell rang in the evening. I was stunned. I walked hastily towards the door. Adrenaline rushed through my body. Had he arrived? I smiled nervously while biting the edges of my lips. If this could happen, then India could be freed from corruption too.

I opened the door and was awestruck. It was him, and my joy knew no bounds. It was a miracle, a dream come true, and I had to make the most of it. So, now I knew, India will be freed from corruption someday.

I smiled and smiled and smiled. I kept staring at him in amazement and excitement. He was drenched by the rain. His white shirt, translucent from being wet, stuck to his chest. He was wearing a pair of blue denims. His left hand was holding a bag and his right one his shoes.

With cold hands and a warm heart, I had opened the door. I don't know why but today I woke up with a smile on my face. I had never invited him over before because the mere thought of my Dad finding out about my love story made me break into a cold sweat. I felt insane and lightheaded.

'Please come in,' I said, and it did not feel like a phrase but some magic enchantment as I gazed at Nishit, looking handsome in his classic white shirt.

The next moment, I saw Shelly, standing behind the big neem tree in our compound, laughing, the literal manifestation of ROFL.

I looked at her and said, 'He must have called you.'

'No, he did not. I came to ruin your date,' she said teasingly.

I quickly asked them to enter before Neena Aunty from the bungalow next door informed the neighbourhood about us at her next kitty party. She had more information about the colony than the US government had about their enemies.

I had told Nishit that my parents were going out of town. While the information was supposed to be an indirect invitation to come over to my place, it still seemed impossible that they had made it.

'Only eighteen days to go for our board exams,' I said.

'So?' Shelly said in her ever-confident style.

'She must be scared,' Nishit said, high-fiving Shelly. 'Don't you know your friend?'

But somewhere deep in my heart, I was happy. And that was the last we talked of exams.

I handed Nishit a white towel and sat on the couch in front of him. The lightning and thunder did not stop. It rained even harder. The curtains were blowing with the wind as if they could also feel the magic around. Suddenly, the electricity went out and the room went dark. The only light was from a small lamp in the corner of the room that was connected to the inverter.

Nishit continued to dry himself with the towel.

'Shall I switch on the other light that is connected to the inverter?' I asked him.

'No,' he replied.

'Isn't that a very concise answer?' I asked.

'Don't you like it this way?' he winked.

'As you wish,' I said with a smile that had been on my lips since the moment I had opened the door.

He started rubbing his head with the towel.

'Why are guys so messy? You don't even know how to use a towel to dry your hair. I pity your hair for having such an arrogant owner,' I giggled.

'But you girls are adept at the art of aesthetics. Just do me a favour! Please teach me how to do all this stuff once I'm your husband,' he laughed.

'It's easy. Let me do it for you. You may also end up learning something, kiddo.' I took slow and steady steps towards him.

The light from the lamp was dim and I had to be careful not to stumble over something. The clouds thundered. As I turned to look out of the window, hoping for a glimpse of lightning, Nishit put his right leg forward. I literally fell for his age-old trick and stumbled to the ground. My back and legs hurt. I hurled abuse at Nishit as loud as I could.

He had not expected me to fall so hard. He was just playing a small prank. I could not move. I told him to help me. He took me in his arms to lead me to the couch. I fastened my hands around his neck, fearing that I would fall again. I looked straight into his eyes, and he looked straight into mine. I could not scold him anymore. His clothes stuck to mine and made them a little wet too.

He firmly placed me on the sofa and sat beside me. He leaned towards me, apologizing for his misdeed. My locks were loosely tied into a bun, except for a few around my face. He pushed them away. Then he moved his hand along my cheek and down my arm to hold my hand as he stared into my eyes.

It reminded me of the play *Romeo and Juliet,* which we had performed for the annual function last year. Except that I was Romeo and Shelly was Juliet. After some role play you realize that you are not acting at all. I had fallen for Shelly at that time. You know, diary! That suddenly made me think of Shelly. Where had she disappeared?

'Are you okay?' he enquired.

'Yeah! I am okay,' I reassured him.

'I didn't mean to hurt you. I could never hurt you. You know that, right?' He seemed guilty for what he had done.

'I know, Nishit. I count on you completely, wholly and dramatically,' I replied.

He smiled then stood up and went to the washroom. When he returned, I saw that he had removed his shirt. In a few seconds, he had stripped off his jeans as well. I had never seen him like that before. He picked up the towel and draped it around his waist. His body still had water droplets scattered all over. He moved towards the kitchen.

'Where do you keep the coffee, Miss?' he called out.

'It's in a brown jar beside the microwave,' I replied.

It was Nishit, and I knew he wouldn't be able to find things even if I gave him the exact location. Sure enough, he returned shortly.

'I did not find it,' he said, walking across to sit beside me.

I did not want to get up, so I exclaimed, 'Is it the coffee or me that you have come to see?' I tried to sound like one of those hopeless romantics.

'And so the gibberish begins,' he teased.

'Don't you love the sound of it?' I winked this time.

'Of course I do,' he said as he leaned towards me.

I was still lying on the couch, but his gesture made me freeze. The only thing I could see was his face, so close, just four inches away from mine. Time ceased as he came closer and the distance between us receded. I saw tears roll down his cheeks and felt them fall on my cheek.

'What's wrong?' I enquired.

'I love you,' he replied.

'I want to wake up to this dream for the rest of my life. I have loved you for ages and will love you till eternity. I just don't understand why you have been keeping me away lately,' I said.

'I am not ready for a commitment yet. But that does not mean I do not care about your emotions,' he said as he ran his fingers through my hair. I hugged him and he clutched me in his arms. I ran my hand down his rib cage and then back up to his neck. I continued doing it as we remained quiet and sat just hugging each other.

'Don't do that,' Nishit said.

'Oh, I'm sorry if you don't like it.' I felt a little self-conscious.

'No. I mean it's turning me on. Don't forget your friend is bare-bodied,' Nishit said.

'Oh no,' I pushed him back.

'What?'

'You'll never change, idiot. I hate you.' I was embarrassed.

'And I love you.'

'So that makes us even!'

'Yeah, sure!'

Shelly came smiling into the living area out of nowhere.

'Where were you all this time?' I asked.

'We have planned a surprise for you. Nishit sent me to the terrace to set it up.'

'What surprise?'

'Surprises aren't told in advance, dumbo!' Shelly said.

Nishit stood up, no longer in his towel, and started walking towards the terrace with Shelly. I got up and followed them.

Much to my amazement, they had planned a movie night. Shelly had borrowed a projector from our science teacher Mr Jain and Nishit had arranged for the DVD. We watched *Home Alone* that night. Intermittent rain did dampen the experience, but we sat there and watched it till the end.

For the three of us, it was my terrace where the sun never set. Not just my terrace; wherever we were, we were inseparable.

Nishit and Shelly had grown closer because of me.

As I saw a shooting star at night, I made a wish. I wanted the three of us to be friends forever. I wanted us to be inseparable.

That's all for now. Good night!

Adios,

Iti

Summer Vacation

6 May 2014

Dear Diary,

Summer vacations are the best, aren't they?

More so when it is the summer vacation that you've been waiting for so long. And guess what? After months of not being able to update you on what is going on in my life, I now have the time to tell you everything about my life again.

So finally, one of the most dreadful years of my school life, the one where I was worried every day about the board exam, has gone by. And the most awaited summer vacation of my life is here.

I am free to roam around, watch TV, go cycling or trekking, meet my friends every now and then.

In India, we do not have the concept of working after school but Riti Didi was telling me that our cousins in the US have taken up summer jobs. I really liked the idea. I spoke with my family, and they were okay with letting me volunteer as a part-time librarian at the Mussoorie Library on Mall Road. My job is to arrange the books after the readers have dropped them off at the reception. If you ask Nishit, he'd say that it is a very menial job, but for me, it is an opportunity to be surrounded by books and therefore I like every bit of it.

It is said that the Mussoorie Library is as old as the city itself. It is at one end of the Mall Road, and I cycle from home to the library every day. Sometimes the roads are full of tourists from Punjab and Delhi, and it takes a little longer than usual to reach there.

Summer is the peak season for tourists. Even the otherwise serene places cease to be so as enormous crowds take over the town. Tourists are a nuisance in Mussoorie sometimes. Their incessant honking disturbs the tranquillity of the hills.

The library is private, and thankfully, tourists are not allowed to enter it. The library is a colonial landmark and its reading rooms and bookcases are full of volumes from an earlier era. I am not being paid a single penny, so they are okay with me taking some days off when I need to. It is kind of a good deal.

The smell of old yellow paper that has turned so fragile that it may decompose on its own much before it can be accidentally torn or burnt by a human makes me happy. It is a feeling of coming back home. I really can't explain what I feel when I hold these books. I want to dive deep into every book and live like the characters for a while. I often have this desire to live many lives. I want to change my name often, be in a different city, get a new job, and make a life distinct from my previous one. I want to keep doing this until I grow old and retire and possibly die. Guess what? If it is true that my soul is that of a writer, I will never retire. My English teacher, Mr Thomas, told me that writers never retire. He visits the library often.

Thomas Sir knows that I want to become a writer. I have told him about my future plans.

He often tells me to break it to my family. He believes that this is the most opportune time. After all, we have to choose which subjects we will pursue in the eleventh and twelfth.

I am so scared, diary. My family wants me to opt for science. Dad was keen on me working at the newly opened cybercafé on the Mall, or trying for an internship at one of the heritage hotels like The Savoy. He believes that learning about technology can do wonders for me in this era.

This is the post-industrial age, he says often. This is the age of computers and the internet. In fact, he is so vested in learning all about computers that he has already bought a new one and hired a tutor to help him understand every bit of it. He often misplaces the research papers he is working on, leading to problems. He is currently working on a hypothesis, and he feels that the computer can become his greatest aide and help him in his research work.

He is correct, though.

My mom has made me speak with Shelly's relatives who live in San Francisco and work for some of the biggest technology companies. They have made a fortune and somehow it is my mom's great Indian dream to send me abroad.

They would both prefer it if I studied computer science.

I want to opt for arts and humanities instead. But I don't know how to convince Mom and Dad. You know what, diary? I secured 98 per cent in English in the pre-boards. Thomas Sir read my essay in front of the whole class and told them that the copy was so perfect he had a hard time figuring out where he should deduct marks.

Whenever Thomas Sir visits the library, we talk for hours about the classics that we've read and loved. The other day we discussed the classic play *Julius Caesar* by William Shakespeare.

Thomas Sir told me, 'You could opt for a degree in mass communication and go to Delhi University. You can also take English as an elective subject then. You could get a job in the field of journalism and try to finish your script in your spare time. You can publish a few books, and once you become successful, you can quit your career in journalism and become a full-time writer. Many writers have done so in the past.'

I told him, 'I want to write for the screen; I don't want to write books.'

He told me, 'Writers can write about anything they want to.'

We shared so many laughs that day. I am so happy that he understands my career choice.

To think about it, Nishit and I have grown really close. Nishit went to meet his maternal uncle's family in Bareilly for a week. Not seeing him for a week made me crazy. He is my life's other routine that I want to keep. He is back now and meets me every evening at Mall Road when I am done with work. We cycle all the way up to Lal Tibba and sit on the bench at the sunrise point. Since it is a sunrise point, not many people visit it during the sunset.

Sometimes he gets us fresh samosas from Lallu Uncle's shop and on other days he gets us popcorn from the Red Little Store. We talk about everything and anything under the sun. It is comforting to sit by his side and spend time with him. I just hope nobody from our families ever gets to know that we're in love. I am glad that they continue to see us as friends.

Shyamala Aunty had once entered the room when we were studying maths and preparing for the board exams. I guess she saw us holding hands, but I am lucky that she hasn't confronted me or anyone else at home about that. I just hope that she continues to mind her own business.

Whenever we could not solve the hard maths problems in the R.C. Verma textbook, Dad would help us navigate the crisis. Nishit is good at maths and that is something that Dad loves about him. I guess he would not mind having an intelligent kid as his son-in-law. I have to marry Nishit. Nothing would make me happier in life.

Shelly has gone to the UK to visit her dad's family, most of whom have settled there along with her grandparents. She was pretty excited as she was travelling abroad for the first time. I can't wait to listen to her London stories when she is back. Also, she will get us presents. Nishit and I are so excited.

Riti Didi is attending college in Dehradun, and she is preparing very hard for her master's. She wishes to go to the US to pursue an MS in computer science. Riti Didi is an average performer, and she could not crack IIT-JEE. Her MS is going to be her revenge against the competitive Indian examination landscape. She wants to prove to the world that one can build a fortune even if one hasn't been to IIT. I guess her biggest revenge will be against Dad, who forced her to get into computer science engineering—just like he is pressuring me now—while she wanted to pursue architecture. She keeps telling me that once she is off, she will never return to India.

Riti Didi is always clear about her choices. She knows exactly what she wants from her life. But unfortunately, that's not true for me.

Nishit also knows about my dreams of becoming a writer, but my family knows nothing about them.

When we had a sex education class in school, our school counsellors had asked us to share any problems we had been facing as teenagers with our family and teachers. But you know what, diary? I feel it is a big sham. Nobody is interested in knowing anybody else's problems. I will have to find my career path on my own.

There are only ten days left before we have to submit our stream of choice for higher secondary school. If I am not able to tell my parents that I don't want to pursue physics, chemistry and maths, I will probably lie to them and I will submit my choice for arts and humanities instead.

Dad has promised to take us on a trekking, camping and sky-gazing adventure. I will try to tell him the truth then.

Life is a drama. One where every year you are told that you have to outperform in exams only this year and then your life will be set. I believe that is the biggest lie being told to students. Every year we are faced with a new challenge, and no year seems to be the last year that you have to put in the effort.

The only place that feels like my own is the Mussoorie Library. People travel to temples, often undertaking arduous journeys to get there, when they need to seek a solution to their problems. I walk into the library. Mussoorie Library is that temple for me!

These are the only events from my not-so-eventful life right now.

Goodbye,

Iti

Another Story

14 April 2020

Dear Diary,

These have been some of the most exhausting days of my life.

I spend most of my time reading my diaries in the outhouse. While many people will recommend that you read some great books, I would strongly recommend reading one's own experiences over the years. It's funny how life is ever-changing and how we are ever-evolving.

We become oblivious to things that matter to us at some point. While some memories fade with time, some bonds grow deeper. While some bonds fade with time, some memories stay forever.

My Facebook friends continued to post exotic recipes while I continued to feed myself Maggi. How much can I bother Shyamala Aunty? The rest of the time

I can't get enough of the Covid-19 tracker that I keep checking again and again like an obsessive maniac.

I thought about trying out Shelly's suggestion and developing a narrative that goes back in time and talks about a similar situation. About how challenges have been a constant in the human journey. That it is just the causing agent that changes. But the story has to be about finding hope in the darkest of times. It should brighten someone's day even during the nights or the rains. The story should be like the terrace where the sun never set for us! We all have a happy place of that sort in the back of our minds.

So here's my new idea. I have refined it a little further. I sincerely hope that Kajol Sir likes it:

Smiti, a young research scholar, is left stranded with other tourists in her late uncle Rick's resort on a remote island in the Andamans due to a sudden worldwide lockdown.

After numerous failed attempts to leave the island, she begins to write *Where the Sun Never Sets* when the resort's ex-caretaker Vanita returns unannounced. She convinces Smiti and the other tourists, Nihaal and Molly (inspired by Shelly), to tell their lockdown survival story to the world.

To give them a semblance of hope, every morning, Vanita insists of telling them stories of the island's past, from the times of the British Raj when it was notoriously called *Kaala Paani*. Every night, Smiti pens a new page of her lockdown survival story in her diary.

With almost no cash, just a few sets of clothing and nothing to brag or show off about, their life becomes unlike anything they had ever imagined, and Vanita, the characters of her stories and Smiti's newfound friends Molly and Nihaal become her only hope to steer her through the pandemic.

As her story progresses, Smiti sees her best memories and worst nightmares come to life. Can travelling to the past give you a clear picture of life? Is planning for the future overrated?

You'll get the answers as you embark on a journey of a lifetime with Smiti, Vanita, Molly and Nihaal.

Will listening to Smiti's story prove to be an adventure? Will life be the same . . . ever?

Period.

I rehearsed my pitch for a long time before setting up a call with Kajol Sir. I guess Prakash Sir will also be a part of the pitch meeting this time. I can't afford for things to go wrong. I even prepped in front of the mirror.

I spent the rest of the day lazing in my pyjamas, watching TV and cooking.

'I just know how to prepare Maggi and mousse. Are you guys up for it?' I called out to Shyamala Aunty and her kids Monu and Shonu. She hasn't been feeling well since yesterday. I have asked her to stay quarantined in her cottage as a precautionary measure.

'Cook anything. We will eat, beta. I am very tired,' she told me.

I walked into the kitchen and searched for some recipes on the internet. Much to my surprise, my social media feed was loaded with Michelin-star chefs now. No, no, I have not started following chefs. But even the laziest guy from my college, Sukku, who knew nothing but emptying whisky bottles, had posted a picture of a dish that he had prepared. God knows how many people Covid-19 will claim in 2020, but obesity and heart disease are going to hit hard five years from now.

I eventually settled on cooking Maggi and mousse!

Entering the kitchen reminded me of Mom. I vividly remember the times when she would prepare my favourite dishes.

I put the dinner for Shyamala Aunty and the kids outside the door to their cottage. Then I came back home and sat to eat alone at the dining table. It reminded me of a conversation I had had with Mom and Dad about my dream of becoming a writer.

'Do you have some story ideas?' Mom asked Dad as we sat at the dining table a few years ago. Why did she do that? She knew that Dad was sceptical about my writing career.

'For Iti's short story competition at school?' he laughed. His classic insult, the lack of respect for my field of interest, drove me crazy on some days. Like it did that day!

'Shut up.' Mom's tone was grave.

'Does Iti know that authors and film writers aren't paid a penny? I was reading the other day in the newspaper—'

'Who reads newspapers?' I interrupted. 'It's the era of digital blogs and digital news.'

'I support our old vendors. They are going out of business due to technology. But forget it. Your self-centred generation would never understand this!'

'Mom, Dad, please don't get started. I don't need your advice. I am a grown-up now. I know how to handle my problems,' I retorted.

'Good to hear that. Both of you are selfish girls.' This came like a bullet out of nowhere. Like the ones fired in the air during Indian weddings that accidentally kill someone. 'Just think about yourself. Reflect,' he continued.

'I think we have acquired it from you.' I left the table and walked towards my bedroom. I walked to you, my diary, my hope. Only you are willing to listen to me. I have trusted you for so long, my confidant.

'Beta! Finish your food first. Papa is always joking,' I heard Mom call out behind me in an attempt to cover up for Dad, but I didn't care to stop.

'Why doesn't he realize that it's very hard for me to live in this home, diary? Why don't they all burn in hell and let me live, diary?' These were the thoughts and questions that surrounded me on that day.

Suddenly, those words from the past reverberated in my mind. It felt like the entire dining space was echoing with those voices. I can't believe that I had wished such evil for my family back then. I couldn't imagine how much I had hated my parents during my teen years.

The only thing I wish today is to have them in my life. I was so stupid back then.

I continued to chew on my Maggi, which was tasteless at that point.

My diary, if it were not for the lockdown I would never have come back to this town.

It is so hard to live with these memories. Every moment, every day suffocates me.

Then, I played some music. Loud music. Shyamala Aunty called me up and warned, 'Lower! Lower! Lower! The neighbours will yell!'

'I don't care anymore!' I replied.

The horizon in life is ever-changing. You can reflect upon the past, often wonder what the future will present. But it's only the present that counts. Not many days ago this present was the future, and not many days from now it will become the past.

Inhale the present, exhale the past.

I slept feeling anxious about making a pitch that gets approved this time. My parents never believed I could be a successful writer. They are no more, but I still need to prove to myself that I can be.

Self-acceptance and validation are still the biggest challenges in my life. I want to be successful. I have never been successful in relationships. I want to be successful in my career at least.

Adieu amigo,

Iti

The New School

1 July 2009

Dear Diary,

Today was my first day at the big new school.

I hate Mom and Dad. They have changed my school from Mt Carmel Girls' High School to Mussoorie Hills International. They did this to Riti Didi first. Does God know why parents always make such stupid decisions?

Relatives feed them irrelevant gyan, and my parents follow their commands like the robots on Cartoon Network that follow human commands. My paternal aunt Pinky told them to transfer me to a co-educational school and they followed her command like cartoon robots.

They also don't let me watch my favourite cartoons on TV. I still love to watch *Gummi Bears*, *TaleSpin*, *DuckTales*, *The Flintstones*, *The Tom and Jerry Show*,

The Jetsons, *The Powerpuff Girls* and *Scooby-Doo! Mystery Inc.*

They tell me, 'You are grown up now and must watch something more informative like the Discovery Channel.'

'I like stories. I don't care about science,' is my typical response.

My grandmother visited us from Raipur last month and she used to tell me all kinds of stories. But now she has gone back, and I have neither the TV nor her stories.

This new school is nonsense too. I had to leave all my good friends back at Mt Carmel. My old school was small, but the students had big hearts.

I have no friends here.

The school is in a huge property on top of a hill. It has many playgrounds and extra-curricular facilities, unlike any other school in town. Every building in the huge six-building complex is painted bottle green and cream and has a red, attic-style roof. The washrooms are huge and clean with mirrors. The only thing I am happy about is that the school has a large library.

What if the library also has some secret chambers, diary? I am yet to go on that mission and find out.

There is a huge cemetery beside the school campus. Many kids in Mussoorie say that ghosts haunt this part of the town after sunset. But the school timings are from 6 a.m. to 2 p.m. so I am safe. The only problem is that the school bus will arrive before sunrise during winters.

I was asked to solve a simple maths problem by my teacher in the class. She literally pointed to me and asked me to introduce myself to the class. Then she asked me to do a sum from the previous standard just to understand what my maths level was. I failed to get the right answer. The entire class laughed and mocked me. Maybe Dad was correct. He needs to hire a maths tutor to help me get better at this subject. He tells me that there is no life without maths.

I once read in a book that the great scientist Albert Einstein once said that you can't judge a fish by its ability to fly. It means that dancers can't be evaluated based on their ability to solve maths sums and mathematicians can't be evaluated based on their ability to move to a rhythm. I tried to explain this to my dad once, but he told me that quotes are good for the books while in real life one has to work hard and learn maths irrespective of anything.

We do not have to carry lunch boxes to school. We are provided with lunch in the mess, and I must say that the food is very tasty. I had my favourite rajma chawal for lunch today.

I sat amidst my classmates in the row that is designated for class six. Most of my classmates have known each other since primary school and they bond with each other so well.

I missed my friend Nikita from my old school.

While coming back on the bus, a very beautiful girl sat beside me. I wanted to talk to her but held myself back due to a lack of confidence. I am full of hesitation, diary.

What can I do?

But she shook my hand and introduced herself as Shelly. She is in sixth class too. She has brown hair and golden eyes. She is the most beautiful girl in my class. She told me that we can be friends and talk to each other every day. She also told me not to worry about what happened in the maths class. She will help me with the sums.

I have promised to help her in the language classes. She struggles with English and Hindi.

She told me that most of her friends left for better schools in Delhi, therefore even she has to make new friends in her old school.

I said thank you to God on my way back home. He has sent Shelly like an angel in my life. I at least have one friend in my new school now.

You know what, diary?

She also told me that she likes Western dance. She will help me choose my elective for extra-curriculars and teach me to dance. I have always loved to dance in front of the TV, but now I will also have a friend-cum-dance teacher.

Thank you, God!

Miss you,

Iti

Never

16 February 2016

Dear Diary,

Valentines' day was a bad day.

Why does every Valentine's Day of my life have to suck? Is it too much to ask for a good date and some gifts?

So as my boring life would have it, I had to invite Shelly over.

God knows why she doesn't accept a proposal from the million proposals she gets on 14 February every year and move on in her life.

At least one of us could then get the Bollywood-like, Hollywood-like, dreamy, breezy, novel kind of day.

'So which movie are we going to watch today?' Shelly asked as she wanted to take my mind off the stupid thoughts I was having. I had shared them with her like I always do.

'No, I don't want to watch a film,' I said, loud and clear.

'You have to! Guess which DVD I managed to get my hands on?' The last time she was so happy she'd managed to get a DVD collection of five romantic movies: *P.S., I Love You*, *If Only*, *Serendipity*, *Sleepless in Seattle*, and *Eternal Sunshine of the Spotless Mind*.

Although I loved them all, *Eternal Sunshine* has got to be my all-time favourite romantic movie. And I so wish that Nishit could make it tonight, and we could watch it together.

'*Fast and Furious*?' I said to tease her. She hates action and adventure.

'No!' She looked at me in disgust.

'*Midnight in Paris*?' I asked as she'd promised to get this one for me. Another classmate of mine had told me that I would love the film because the protagonist was a writer who she felt was a little crazy like me.

'No,' she grinned.

'Shelly, please don't tell me you've gotten another blue film from some random backbencher. I have promised myself that I won't ever watch that sinful stuff.' It occurred to me that Shelly felt that she was grown-up enough now and wanted to try all the crazy stuff adults do. Shelly could go to any extent to make her bucket list come true.

'Don't worry. It is not exactly that. We're going to watch *American Pie*.'

'Shelly. Please. I am in no mood to watch all that nonsense. I have heard from classmates that it is kind of a bad film.'

'Why are you so upset all the time?' she frowned.

'This is probably the last Valentine's Day that Nishit and I can spend together, Shelly. Why did he have to go to Bareilly?' I asked her helplessly.

'He couldn't have postponed his grandmother's death to be with you. I am here with you. I always will be. You don't have to be upset. I got this DVD to entertain you,' she said as she walked over to place it in the DVD player.

My family is out to attend a wedding in Jaisalmer. I was spared as I am appearing for the boards, and my parents wanted me to stay cloistered and mug up as many books as I could. Parents' fantasies of their kids are no short of a romantic Hollywood film.

'Okay, let's watch it,' I said reluctantly.

'Do you have some drinks in the bar cabinet?' she asked.

'No. No Shelly. It was only once that we tried it.'

She slipped her hands into her pink school bag and pulled out a bottle of wine.

'Where did you get that?' I freaked out.

'I sent my older brother to get it,' she winked.

'I am not having it.' I turned my back to her as I sat on the corner of my bed.

'Come on. Chill. Let's have some.' She sat beside me and placed her hand on my shoulder.

I always give in to her ideas. I am the boring one, you know my diary.

'Okay,' I muttered.

We played the movie in my room. A couple of hours and a few drinks down we felt a little tipsy. Shelly suggested that we dance to our favourite songs like there's no tomorrow. I said yes. A little wine could always do that magic to me. I was transformed into an exciting person!

They say that alcohol often brings out our true side.

She wrapped her arms around my neck and played our favourite song from the iconic movie *Titanic*. As the song played in the background, the distance between us receded. Soon her lips were pressed against mine and we kissed each other passionately, unendingly.

I always held myself back from kissing Nishit, but at that very moment, kissing Shelly did not feel wrong. We crashed on to my bed and passed out after that. Or maybe I have no memory of what happened later.

When I woke up the next morning she had already left. When I entered the bathroom and looked into the mirror, I felt ashamed of myself for kissing a girl.

I slapped myself and brushed my teeth as hard as I could. I tore my clothes into pieces and later burnt them. I bathed and scrubbed myself so hard it was as if I wanted to remove my skin.

My biggest fear was confronting Nishit. What was I going to tell him, diary? Would he forgive me ever, diary? Is this also considered cheating, diary?

After all, I have always loved him. But I could sense that Shelly had a crush on me. She is into girls. She is a lesbian.

I called her up, but she did not answer.

The next day I asked her to meet me after our classes on the school grounds. She came to see me as promised. She wanted to hug me, but I pushed her away. I slapped her and asked her to never show her face to me again. At least not in this life.

It felt so wrong, it felt so right. It did help me get into revenge mode, for a moment at least!

But later I had to lie to Nishit and every other student in class. 'How could we not be friends anymore?' This question haunted me like a ghost. The whole school knew we were inseparable.

I had to make up all sorts of shit like she broke my trust. Blah blah blah. And so much more. I am also the one who started the rumour about her being a lesbian.

This week has been stressful in particular. I feel so lonely and lost. My stupid decisions could have made me lose my best friend forever. But I don't care.

I am so spiteful, and I want to ruin her for what she did to me.

Alvida,

Iti

The City

3 July 2018

Dear Diary,

I feel like I have lost touch with reality these days.

One needs to move away from family to grow in life. Even if it means growing apart from your loved ones, or their memories. And I took all these necessary steps when I moved into this new apartment in Gurgaon.

That's what Riti did first. You know that. She moved out of India when I needed her the most. Now, she lives alone in her studio apartment in the US.

In the first-ever company party that I attended, my seniors asked me to stand on a table and sing in front of the new batch. I was nervous, shy, lacking confidence and not so sure about what I wanted from my life. This was no surprise as when I was in Mussoorie, I was always in a cocoon, pampered by my family.

The struggle of living alone is real. Everything that's happening will mould me into a better version of myself. Every incident, good or bad, defines me and is significant to my existence. I am confident, passionate and clearer about my choices now. But it's a journey and it never happens overnight.

Unlike humans, the tree doesn't know many colours. It is green everywhere and offers you the same comfort. But it isn't so here. Women are disadvantaged even in these huge towers. Foreigners get a preference when we discuss appraisals.

Life isn't as simple as it was in Mussoorie.

But my flatmate Anvika tells me that soon I will be accustomed to this 'new normal'. We are always adjusting to some 'new normal'.

She reminds me of Dad, who believed the same thing but chose different words to communicate the message: 'Change is the only constant'.

I have dated a few guys. I found them via apps. None of them loved me as Nishit did, or Shelly did.

I have become bolder than I was back in my hometown. I have also slept with a few guys, but they never asked me if I was satisfied, never cared about me. Ironically, I never slept with the one who loved me and here I am desperately seeking someone who can love me.

The guys that I have met have been my gateway to momentary happiness. With them, it is just about having sex. I have never been lonelier in life, diary! I crave a real sense of belonging in a relationship. I long to be loved and cared for!

I read an interesting blog by my favourite blogger Ramy. He said that kindness comes back to us only if we choose to be kind at every step in life. I recently flew all by myself in an aircraft. I bought a meal for the lady sitting next to me. We exchanged numbers and promised to catch up sometime in Gurgaon.

But she's super busy. She never called. If I ever meet Ramy, I am going to tell him that kindness does not necessarily return. But maybe you still have to choose to be kind as a way of life.

Pretension is at its peak here. People judge the outermost layer of a person by what they wear and how they smell. Work is just a way to keep me busy. In the end, all that I desire is to take the journey to self. I feel I will be able to realize it only when I get a chance to write my own story someday.

Months will change into years. Will I ever be able to make a move, diary? Life is rotten, stagnant and almost non-existent.

I messaged Ramy on Instagram a few days ago. He did write back to me. 'Treat others, love others, the way you wish to be loved.'

I am living by his words. Trying to do the best I can. I hope I will be able to get over this loneliness sometime soon. I don't have a lot to write about.

Sometimes, I wish you could talk. Tell me something. Advise me.

My parents are no more. My sister doesn't care. I lost my only friends. If there were a trophy for the biggest loser in the world, it could be given to me.

My therapist, Poonam Malwani, suggests speaking with the five people I am closest to. But I seem to have lost them all. Some to death. Some to bad choices.

When I told her about you, she was glad that I at least maintain a journal. I met her again sometime back.

She lectured me non-stop. While at first I didn't believe in a lot of things she told me, slowly and steadily, I am giving in to her confidence. She is the only one who understands and empathizes with me. She truly believes what happened with my family is not justified. She has diagnosed me with post-traumatic stress disorder or PTSD for short. She says I will be over it soon. I will have to try harder though.

Also, she has asked me to write everything down in a diary so I remember the stuff she tells me. She mentored me to become a storyteller and follow my inner calling.

'Do what you love and everything else follows,' she suggested.

'You can make others happy only if you are happy from within. Think about what you want to own ten years down the line. It is okay to be happy with a car or a bungalow if that's what you want. It would get more complicated with time if it is actually something that you don't want. Every person has a story, and it is their journey that sets them apart from others.'

'I just want to be successful. I am sick of failing at life. I want to build a career and get loads of money in my bank account,' I told her about my ambitions.

'You need not be wealthy to be successful. Success isn't measured in terms of money. It can be measured only in terms of whether or not you were able to do what you wanted to do. Write your dream movie script. It will give you a sense of accomplishment,' she stressed.

'I am alone. I have no one to pat me on my back,' I shared my fear with her.

'Questions are the face of fear but remember that on the other side of fear lies freedom.'

Though she uttered many more words of wisdom that day, her final words left me puzzled, intrigued, speechless yet thoughtful.

'Do you think that Mahatma Gandhi or Warren Buffet are the only successful people? They are for sure, but there are quite a few successful people around you as well, it's just that you see them but do not notice them. Who in your circle do you think is happy, satisfied and successful? Your teacher, friends, relatives?'

When she asked me this question, much to my amazement, I could not think of anyone, including myself. All of them had wanted something, but they were trapped in the rat race and ended up doing something completely different. All of them had enough money, but none of them ever seemed satisfied with what they did. Lightning struck me as I finally thought of a name and had an answer. I didn't have the guts to speak it aloud as it somehow pinched my ego more than anything else. But on my way back home later I could still see only one name that flashed again and again in my mind. Shyamala Aunty.

'I will have to find the courage to write my story someday. I will have to quit my job. I will have to move back to Mussoorie. But I can't move back to that city. There's nothing left for me there now,' I told Poonam.

'You will have to accept that what has happened has happened. You will have to move back, my dear. Take your time,' she said.

I kept quiet for a few minutes.

She showed me a chart and asked me to point out the emotions I was feeling right then.

I pointed to sadness, fear, disgust, jealousy and anger one by one to give her a visual tour of my mind.

She then explained to me, 'On having lost loved ones in our life we go through five stages of grieving—denial, anger, bargaining, depression and acceptance. Everybody spends a different amount of time in each stage.'

She further explained to me, 'After two years you have reached the stage of anger. I will help you reach acceptance. You are not alone, and I am with you on this journey.'

'Will I have to go through depression?' I asked her.

'It is not necessary that a patient experiences every stage linearly or goes through every stage.' She reached out across the table to hold my hand and reassure me that she would be by my side no matter what.

She continued, 'I am glad that you've shared your diary entries with me. But many parts feel like your version of the story. They are inconsistent with your real confessions during our sessions.'

'I do write my version of the story. I do so to cope with the situation. My stories give me hope.'

'But this behaviour shows that you're still in the denial and bargaining stages of your journey. You are not ready to accept the past, let alone make peace with it.'

'I don't see a problem in maintaining my version of the stories in my diary.'

'You're a writer and you must pen down fictional accounts separately. You must label it as fiction in your diary as well as your head. What concerns me is the fact that you might unknowingly become a compulsive liar. To be unable to distinguish between fact and fiction in real life could have serious repercussions on the quality of your life.'

'Umm . . . hmm,' was the only thing I could utter.

She wanted to break our bond, diary. You never asked me to be truthful, did you? Do you have a problem with my sharing my version of the story with you and not the facts? Tell me?

She is intruding in every sphere of my life. But Shyamala Aunty and my college counsellor Arun Verma Sir want me to keep visiting her to heal. Shyamala Aunty keeps checking on me by calling me from Mussoorie. She really loves me a lot.

When I came back home, I realized that I have to visit Poonam frequently until I can get over my past. I am hopeful that I will come out of depression someday. There has to be light at the end of the tunnel. My story has to have a happy ending, diary.

Please don't disown me ever, diary. I love you the most.

Lots of love,

Iti

The Call

17 April 2020

Dear Diary,

Today was the best day since the lockdown was announced.

This new reality is agonizing. I have lost track of time living all on my own for days and days. I have read so many diaries. I have read so many books as well. I think the refined version of the idea that I have now will be appreciated by Kajol Sir.

But I am not very confident, my diary. I have become the kind of person who gets 'better luck next time' a hundred times in a row.

While I believe time never really moves if you stay in the same place, it does. Guess what? The rose that I planted on my balcony has bloomed. It is a reminder that we all have limited time. The flower's time is limited in front of you, but you don't realize that even your time is limited in the vast timeline of the universe.

So it is untrue that time stood still. Even as I sat by myself day after day, the buds bloomed into beautiful flowers. The rains deepened the colour of my surroundings, washing away the dirt, and a bird's eggs hatched in the nest in the tree outside my window. Without meaning to, I had started living in the moment, making the most of this momentary existence.

Happiness derived from existing isn't ephemeral. It seems to last forever. My skin glows like fireflies and my mind is focused like a hermit's. Lockdown is not that terrifying after all. I have started finding peace in my own company. I don't need a lot of people to keep me happy all the time. My expectations from life are now so low that it's almost impossible to not satisfy me.

Now I am going to share my new idea with you. I have finally taken everyone's suggestion to keep the story relatable and real. Here's the new, and short but sweet, idea that I am going to pitch:

Where the Sun Never Sets

A story about finding hope in the darkest of times that will brighten your day!

If you find someone's diary, would you dare open it?

Well, if you chance upon your old diary, would you dare read through your past?

Iti moves back to her hometown amidst a worldwide lockdown to work on her first-ever movie script. Iti's chance encounter with her first love Nishit, her reunion with her estranged best friend Shelly, and the nights she spends reading her well-kept diaries make her best memories and worst nightmares come to life. She has been running away from her past, but now has no choice but to face it.

Will reading her old diaries prove to be an adventure worth taking to complete the script? Will life be the same? Ever?

Set against the backdrop of the great lockdown of 2020, *Where the Sun Never Sets* is a riveting personal account of unforgettable childhood dreams, turbulent teenage years, complicated relationships, human resilience, and the never-ending journey of growing up.

Yes, this is my plot summary. I know you would have liked it, my love, my diary.

I called Kajol Sir. Prakash Sir was also on the Zoom call. I told them all about my idea. I didn't pause for even a minute. It felt like I had had multiple shots of a drug. I felt my passion flow out in words.

Deep within, I know that my story is my plan of redemption. While I cannot go back into my past and change things, I can do so in my story, my world. And that gives me a renewed sense of belief in myself.

'I love it, it is a brilliant idea,' Prakash Sir said when I finished. 'When can I have the full script?'

'In about a month,' I replied cheekily.

'Is there a love angle between the characters?' Prakash Sir enquired.

'Yes there is!' I replied.

'Is it between the characters Iti and Nishit?'

'Yes. But not just them. It is kind of a love triangle.'

'Love triangles are so boring. Two girls after a guy. Eventually, he keeps one and he leaves one.'

'No Sir. Shelly and Nishit both love Iti. Iti loves Nishit.'

'I like that you've got an LGBTQ angle to the story. Who finally wins her over?'

'Iti and Nishit are going to be together. It is a happy ending, Sir,' I reassured him.

'This sounds brilliant. Make Shelly and Iti settle. Or just make sure that you give Shelly closure with some side character. Probably another girl. We can't leave any character unhappy. Indian audiences want a happy ending,' Prakash Sir reiterated.

'Yes Sir. Kajol Sir keeps reminding me about the same. I will keep that in mind.'

'We have also asked a few others to present,' Kajol Sir informed me. 'We will make the final decision only after reading everyone's complete script.'

'Okay Sir,' I smiled. 'I will try my best.'

Kajol Sir is as organized as a pack of Pringles. I need to work my ass off to impress him, diary! God knows what my other colleagues are up to.

'People like mystery. They want the model to put some clothes on rather than stay nude. Have some kind of mystery in this script,' Prakash Sir added.

'I will try my best,' I said.

But where do I bring in the mystery now, diary? I was told to write a feel-good script. What the heck? Why do people want everything out of a poor writer? Why are we supposed to follow so many parameters? Despite all of that, why do most writers die poor?

In spite of that twist, today was one of the best days since the lockdown began. I can't believe that I finally have my much-needed validation.

Now it's time to get back to the outhouse and read more entries from my diaries. Finally, I have gathered the courage to dive back and read from the diary of 2016.

I sincerely believe that my tragic past could become an interesting subplot. My family members could become characters in my story.

Poonam Malwani once told me that as a storyteller I had the magical power to transform every experience as per my wish. I could always give my stories the endings that I may have wanted.

Super excited,

Iti

The Adventure

24 May 2014

Dear Diary,

How excited are you, my love?

I am very excited today and so you must be too. After all, I have brought you to the woods, and I am camping under the stars just like I had always imagined.

I am writing in you from no other place but the George Everest Peak in Mussoorie. While there is a motorable road all the way up here, and I have come to this place before, we did not come here in Dad's car today.

So? Who is with me? How did I reach here, diary?

Be patient, I am going to tell you everything, just like I always do.

Remember I mentioned that Dad had promised to take us camping under the stars after our board exams, diary?

Yes, this is it. We're on 'that' trip.

Jay really wanted to come along, but Dad has promised to take him on such trips after two years when he is as old as I am. So, it is Dad, Riti Didi, Shelly, Nishit and I who have come on this trip.

We assembled at Gandhi Chowk on Mall Road at 6 a.m. and hiked 6 km in four hours to reach one of the famous attractions in the Tehri Garhwal region of the Himalayan Shivaliks: the mansion of Sir George Everest, also known as Park Estate. He was a British surveyor and geographer who served as Surveyor General of India from 1830 to 1843.

The trail ran through a dense forest of oak and cedar trees as well as along grassy hillsides. The panoramic view of the mighty Himalayas was worth every ounce of energy spent in making the hike.

We have carried all the essentials in our backpacks. We are so prepared that we can face the apocalypse. We had a wonderful picnic-type breakfast on reaching and then we erected our white tents just in front of Park Estate.

Not everyone can camp here, but Dad is a rock star as he gets these kinds of permissions easily. Dad works on government projects apart from serving as a full-time senior faculty member and as the dean of the physics department at the Dehradun Technological University.

One of the many interesting side projects he has been working on is converting Sir George Everest's mansion, which the geographer used as an observatory-cum-home from 1832 to 1843, into an observatory for tourists.

Later at 12 p.m., when the sun and its scorching light had hit its peak, we went up to the George Everest Peak, which is just 500 metres uphill from Park Estate. That part of the hike was the most challenging. There is no proper path and one has to trek up the rough and steep mountain slope.

It took us thirty minutes to reach the summit. We saw breathtaking views of Doon Valley on one side and the Aglar River Valley and the snow-capped Himalayan Range to the north. The Gangotri glacier was visible as one of the snow-capped peaks from here. Dad helped us catch closer views with the help of his high-powered binoculars.

Dad broke the silence that filled the air apart from the occasional wows that came out of our mouths, 'The Gangotri glacier is one of the primary sources of the Ganga River and is one of the largest in the Himalayas.'

'We should do this more often, Uncle,' Nishit said as he literally jumped in joy after catching a glimpse of the glacier. I have never seen him so happy. Dad can adopt him and both of them can talk about the sun, stars and sky till eternity.

The view was breathtaking and the journey back adventurous. I slipped twice and fell once. Thankfully, not in the valley. Nishit or Dad held my hand for most of the way back. Shelly and Riti Didi are good at trekking. They taught me how to balance my body weight so as not to fall on my back while descending a steep slope.

We returned to our camp at 2 p.m. and had lunch. A furry *pahadi* dog named Tiger came to us and befriended us. He guards a Maggi and tea stall that caters to tourists and is just outside the main gate of Park Estate. His owner, Mahesh Uncle, told us his name.

Dad asked us to take a break until sunset because the real sky-gazing would only begin after sunset. He said we could sleep or read a book or just go round and round around the trees chasing each other or Tiger.

We did all of it!

As sunset approached and we gathered near the viewpoint, Dad said, 'Tonight is a new moon night. The night sky is going to be very dark, making it easier for us to spot the stars, constellations and the Milky Way. The light from the moon is so strong on some nights that it makes it difficult to stargaze and therefore a new moon night has been specially chosen as the night for camping. Are we excited?'

'Yes,' the group shouted in unison.

The sunset behind the mighty mountain range was spectacular. The three of us sat next to each other, and Tiger accompanied us. Riti Didi was busy setting up the equipment for tonight's show with Dad.

The three of us sat atop a huge rock beside the viewpoint. Shelly held my hand. I held Nishit's hand. It happened in such sync that I felt for a moment that it was telepathy.

Has it ever happened to you that someone knows exactly what you are thinking without you having spoken a single word? Has it ever happened to you that you and your friend end up humming the same tune at the same time? Has it ever happened to you that you were miles away from your mom but knew on that day she was unwell even without her telephoning you?

Life is mysterious, isn't it, diary?

While it is human to try and find an answer and reason for everything through research and science, the truth is that it is the little mysteries that surround us that make us experience the emotions that make us feel alive in the truest sense, in a way that facts will never be able to!

'I feel this has happened before,' Shelly said as she broke our silence.

'What?' Nishit asked.

'The three of us, sitting here, next to each other,' Shelly replied.

'You're experiencing déjà vu,' I told her.

'Yes, I am.'

'You know, one of the theories suggests that déjà vu happens because there are multiple universes, and we are living a life in each one of them. So when we feel that something has happened to us here, it could have actually happened to a different version of us in one of the other universes. Hence, that feeling!' I explained.

'You and your conspiracy theories,' Nishit laughed as he added, 'Have you started working on a science fiction novel yet?'

'No. Not really. She is so scared of telling her dad that she doesn't want to pursue science but possibly write science fiction,' Shelly exclaimed.

'I don't know how to tell him,' I said in a helpless tone.

'We will tell him tonight, don't you worry, child,' Nishit said as he high-fived Shelly.

'Counting on you,' I said as I felt a little relaxed that I wouldn't have to face Dad all on my own.

'The equipment is set up,' Dad shouted out to us. 'Come soon!'

The sky was clear and we wanted to stay up all night and never go to sleep.

The first star, the North Star, popped up in all its glory even before the sky was completely dark. And then, one after the other, like little sparkles from the fire that burnt in front of the tents behind us, stars came to light. In no time, the sky was full of stars. The starlight reflected from the white snow-capped mountains was poetry. Being a lover of the stars, the moon, the galaxies, tonight was a truly memorable night for me.

We had our dinner at 9 p.m. Driver Uncle, who is Shyamala Aunty's husband, drove Mom and Jay all the way up so they could join us for dinner.

'Iti wants to be a writer,' Nishit broke the silence as everyone was busy having the delicious rajma chawal prepared by Shyamala Aunty and Mom.

'What?' Dad looked surprised. 'Iti never mentioned this to us.'

Jay nodded with a smile as he knows about this, just like you, my diary. I tell Riti Didi many things, but I feared sharing this with her as she gets judgemental just like Dad about anyone who does not want to pursue mathematics or science. She looked quite shocked.

'Royalties don't pay the bills,' Dad said, clear, crisp and loud.

'I know, Dad. I want to pursue mass communication and take up a job in the field of journalism or writing. I will publish my first book or maybe finish my first movie script and only when I have achieved success will I take it up full-time,' I said like a robot. I was indeed a robot and my English teacher Thomas Sir had programmed me and helped me figure out this career path.

'We will see,' was all Dad said.

Nobody uttered a word after that.

Shelly would have stood up for me had it been anyone else, but she dreaded raising her voice in front of my dad. She knew that if he got to know that she plans to pursue fashion, he would try to talk her out of it without understanding her point of view.

The only person Dad is happy about is Nishit because becoming a pilot involves studying mathematics and physics. But I was happy that he did not compare me with Nishit or Riti Didi like on every other occasion. He seemed to have made peace with the fact that his daughter wants to pursue arts and humanities, no matter what.

Dad had forgotten some equipment at home and therefore asked Driver Uncle to come back tomorrow evening and drive Riti Didi and him back home so they could pick it up.

After we bid adieu to Mom and Jay, we returned to our viewpoint and started our hunt for the stars from the most distant galaxies.

Did you know about this, diary?

The earth is part of the solar system that is in turn part of the Milky Way galaxy. We stayed awake till 2 a.m. to catch the clearest view of our galaxy. And we did. It was like poetry that can't be expressed in words but the intensity of which can be felt on the darkest of nights.

Look at me, I have turned out to be a night owl. I need to catch some sleep and therefore it's time to say bye to you. Everyone else is fast asleep. And Tiger is guarding us tonight like a guardian angel. I need to kiss him good night too.

That's how we concluded a spectacular day one. I can't wait to see what tomorrow holds for us. We plan to be here for three long days after all!

Until next time,

Iti

The Dream

25 May 2014

Dear Diary,

Today was the scariest day of my life.

Today was day two of our camping adventure. Just pinch me and tell me that everything that I am going to write about is not reality but just a dream.

As dusk fell, Nishit, Shelly and I decided to go further along the road that runs by our camping place near Sir George Everest's house. It was my idea. I had heard at school that there is a huge cemetery at the end of this less-travelled road. Our seniors often dare each other to walk the road at night.

Most of these stories that trend in our school are made up by our seniors. In fact, Shelly and I believe that there is one such story trending on the campus of every school in India. Our school is on top of a hill surrounded by hills and forests. The campus is from the colonial era, hence it is an obvious place for our great grand seniors to start a story from.

We challenged each other to walk to the end of the road, scream our names out loud into the valley, and walk all the way back to the campsite. Since Dad and Riti Didi had gone to get the stuff we had forgotten at home, we had a huge window to perform our daring stunt.

The last words that Dad had uttered were, 'Do not step out of the camp,' to which the three of us had agreed in unison, 'Yes!'

But we had planned this even before Dad had planned the camping trip. The only variable for us was when we would take up this challenge.

I forgot to tell you. There was also a rumour at school that whoever completes this frightening walk is blessed by God and therefore scores top marks in the board exams.

While we know that this does not make any sense, we were willing to take the risk for the sake of our ranks. We wanted to be the top performers.

Nishit asked, 'Are you sure we should do this?'

'Why not! Are you scared already?' Shelly teased him.

'I thought you were the bravest of all of us, Nishit,' I added.

'I mean, I am not really scared of ghosts, but wild animals scare me. My only concern is that we aren't prepared enough for the situation. It's not the city, it's the woods,' Nishit said.

'I am not afraid of the dark. I am not scared of the animals or the height even,' Shelly said. 'I am just afraid of water. Had this hunt been inside water, I would have withdrawn long ago.'

'I am afraid of anything and everything under the sun,' I told them as I started to re-evaluate our decision to go off in the dark.

'Let us try it out once and for all,' Nishit said, 'just don't act like damsels in distress if we are faced with any real danger.'

'We can always run back to our camp,' I said as I raised my hand for a team high-five. They joined me.

We took our torches, water bottles, a knife, a wristwatch and some apples.

We started to walk along the road. It was bordered by a dense forest on each side, making anything beyond two feet invisible. Mussoorie is enveloped in fog during the evenings. The fog was not very dense as it was summertime; had it been wintertime, it would have been impossible for us to walk or drive on the road at night.

The roads in Mussoorie city, like Mall Road, are adorned with huge Victorian-style lamp posts on either side, making the path visible even on the darkest and coldest of nights. But on the road we were taking, light is almost non-existent.

We turned on our torches and with nothing but courage in our hearts started to march towards our destination. Our eyes were focused on the ground, and we took cautious steps.

We walked for about five or seven minutes. To be honest, dear diary, I had lost track of time. I didn't know about Shelly and Nishit, but I had been chanting the Gayatri Mantra in my mind. And there was a point when I wanted to give up and tell them to continue. But then I thought about walking back to the camp all alone and realized that was scarier than my current situation. So I asked my emotional mind to shut up and listen to my logical mind.

I pointed my torch at Shelly. She had been leading the way. She was walking in front of me. I was in the middle.

I asked her softly, 'Isn't this a pointless pursuit? I am scared that my dad will get back before us and he will stop taking us out on these adventure trips. Don't you think it is wiser to head back to the camp?'

'What?' she said as she looked behind. She seemed to agree with me as she pointed her torch in front of her just like me. 'Nishit, what do you think?'

Before Nishit could say a word, I interrupted, 'Shelly, have you lost your mind?'

'Why?' She turned back to me.

'Nishit has been walking behind me all this time,' I said.

'So who is walking in front of me?' she said as she pointed her torch in front of her again, this time lifting it high enough to be able to see until the end of the road that took a sharp left turn.

There was no one. Her face turned pale as she turned back and grabbed my hand. We turned around and started walking quickly towards the camp. Both of us were too scared to talk. It was only after we had taken about twenty steps that I said, 'Where is Nishit?'

'He wasn't ahead of me, I know that now, and he is not behind us. We need to reach the camp soon and alert the adults and start looking for him,' she said, panting.

I took a deep breath as I said, 'Are you sure you could see till the end of the road?'

'Yes,' she replied.

We walked as fast as we could. We got back to the camp and were luckily unharmed.

'You stay, I am going to find him,' Shelly said as I entered the tent.

'No. Please don't go alone. It is scary out there. Let us wait for my dad and we will all go to look for him in the car,' I said as I held her hand.

I was so scared at this point that I could not imagine, understand, process or say anything.

'I have to go. What if he has been attacked by a wild animal?' she yelled at me.

'Then why did we come back in the first place? We should have stayed there, right?' I yelled back at her as I clutched her hand even tighter.

'Iti, you are the writer-type. You overimagine everything. I know how shit-scared you were back there. I wanted to rescue you first from the situation,' she said as she left.

I saw her walking away quickly. She grew smaller and smaller in perspective as I watched her from the little window in the tent. I wanted to go with her, but I was so scared that I could not move my limbs. I felt that I was helplessly frozen in one place and I had nowhere to escape. All I wanted to do at that moment was give my mom a tight hug.

Why are we faced with such situations in life? Did I feel guilt for having suggested that stupid idea to my friends? I had put both of their lives in danger because of a stupid suggestion. I deserved to be lost and not either of them. I broke into tears. I kept sobbing for about fifteen minutes. I could see neither Shelly nor Nishit nor Dad driving back in his red little car.

I had never felt lonelier.

Shelly and Nishit returned to the camp after almost twenty minutes. I looked at my wristwatch more than two hundred times all this while.

As they entered the camp, I saw that Nishit had a bruised hand and a broken nose. He was bleeding from the multiple cuts on his body. His yellow t-shirt was slightly torn on one side.

I ran towards him and hugged him, 'Sorry, love,' were the only words that came out of my mouth.

Shelly searched our bags for our first aid kit. She started dressing his wounds as I sobbed. Nishit sat in silence. He did not utter a word. God knows what had happened to him.

'Where did you find him?' I asked Shelly.

'I found him in the bushes on the left side of the path just five minutes from here. He had accidentally stumbled over a stone and fallen on the other side. He was knocked unconscious and lay there for quite some time. When I found him, I poured the water from my bottle on him. He woke up. He somehow gathered the strength to get up as I helped him. We walked slowly all the way back,' Shelly said.

'"Thank you" were the only words that came out of his mouth,' Shelly added.

I cried and cried and cried more than I had ever before, more than I had ever known I could. Nishit sat there stone cold. He did not say anything. Maybe he was too scared to say a word that night.

When Dad and Riti Didi came back, Shelly told them the entire story. Our trip ended right there. We wrapped up everything, put it in the back of the car and drove them home first, then went to our home.

I have been grounded for some time and so are both of my friends. I called Nishit up and he said he is doing fine. He just needs some time off. He is in a state of shock.

Does God know what is going to happen next? I just pray to Him that our lives get back to normal soon. Or maybe some new normal where our parents will have a completely new way to regulate our whereabouts. Why is life such hell for kids? We are always adjusting to some 'new normal' set by our families.

Good night!

Iti is feeling shitty . . .

The Nightmare

17 October 2016

Dear Diary,

It's been quite some time since I shared things with you. Honestly, it has been the most challenging time of my life.

One year into college and I had finally started enjoying life. I had finally started moving on after my break-up with Nishit. I had finally started making new friends, one of whom could potentially replace Shelly.

But last month I received the most horrible news of my life, my diary. What can I tell you? I have been unable to talk to anyone since.

Why did God punish me? Why did this happen to them? Why did this happen to my family? Why not anyone else?

It's unbelievable how we become sadists in times of grief. We want the world to suffer just because we are suffering. The human mind works in insane ways.

I still can't forget the day I received the news. My hands tremble as I pour my heart out to you, diary. I did not even feel like doing so until my college counsellor Arun Verma Sir suggested that I start writing my daily diary again.

And here I am. I want to tell you everything that I could not in the past few months.

I was in college here in Delhi. Jay was going to give his SAT exam and his centre was in Delhi. Mom and Dad decided to come with him. They also wanted to meet me as they hadn't seen me since I had started college. Shyamala Aunty's husband, our Driver Uncle, was driving them.

And . . .

The car crashed into the valley. Nobody survived the accident. I can't stop crying, diary. I feel like I should have been in that car. How can they all die?

If I die today, will I get to meet them? In heaven, maybe. Life is hell without them.

Riti Didi never came back. She doesn't even call me. She has made peace with the fact that they are no more. She doesn't want to come back to India. I have no one. I just have you, my diary.

I hope I will get past this soon. I do not have the courage or the energy to write more. I don't even have the energy to get out of bed on most days.

I don't feel like going back to Mussoorie ever. I will never go back.

I will just keep moving ahead in life. To new cities, new places. I will build a life like Riti Didi did.

Can life get worse, my diary? Will I ever be able to get past this, my diary? Should I even live, my diary?

Will I ever have the courage to share my story with the world? Will I ever be able to realize my dream of becoming a writer?

Life sucks. Life is hell. Life is a piece of shit.

Is it okay to sometimes feel that I don't want to live anymore, diary?

After leaving for college, I never spoke to Nishit. I haven't seen Shelly since. But I have heard that she's moved abroad to pursue her bachelor's in fashion just like she had always dreamt. She is in Milan. I am happy for her.

I have never been lonelier. I don't have anyone to share my sorrows with! I miss Jay too. Whenever Riti Didi was not around Jay was with me. Jay was always there. Jay was my favourite sibling.

I have lost the will to survive, my diary. Arun Verma Sir says that we all have to find meaning in life. My life stands meaningless as of now.

I can go on and on. But I have lost the energy to share as well. Sometimes, I am locked in my hostel room for hours. I stare at inanimate objects like the ceiling fan, the wooden cupboard, my roommate's bed.

Everyone has been trying to help me, but they seem to have lost patience now. They must feel I am crazy. My college mates must think I am a weirdo.

Life doesn't seem to get better. Why did God spare my life?

Can't write more,

Iti

The Future

5 September 2015

Dear Diary,

Today my heart felt heavy with the burden of unsaid words for the first time.

Why do your siblings have to part ways with you in life? Has it occurred to you that life would be so much more beautiful if we could always stay close to the ones we love?

Dad keeps saying that change is the only constant. But my only question is, why is change the only constant?

A week ago I woke up to the most upsetting news of the year. Riti Didi has cleared the interview for a master's in computer science from one of the good universities in the US, the University of Chicago. She is going to Delhi next week, from where she will fly to the US. I am happy for her, and I will always want her to get the best in life. I am just so upset about the situation.

She'll move. In not more than a year's time, Nishit, Shelly and I will move. Why? Why do we have to separate in the first place? Can't we stay with each other, love each other, take care of each other and always be in Mussoorie?

What if an apocalypse is about to hit, and we are all forced to live together? Would we still want to move out to build a better life?

Why does our future hold so many uncertainties? Why does life have to be hard all the time?

These days are full of gloom. Every passing day is a reminder of the impending doom. When I feel low, I sometimes visit the Mussoorie Library where I did my summer job. They still love me and welcome me.

I don't feel like sharing anything with anyone. I find my peace in the books that I read there. I don't really feel like opening up.

When I read books I want to go back to the past. I am not at all the kind of person who looks forward to the future. I am soaked from head to toe in an eternal sense of gloom because of this impossible desire. I want to keep walking back in time and live the most beautiful moments of my life all over again.

The thought of moving to the city and building a life of my own is also scary as hell. Most of my classmates are so enthusiastic about moving out of their hometown to build a dream life that I sometimes wonder why I am the only one who doesn't really feel so. I want to hold on to the present. I sometimes feel that no matter where I go in life, I will never be able to take Mussoorie out of me.

Yesterday, we had arranged a farewell party for Riti Didi. Nishit and Shelly also joined us. Some of our family friends from in and around town also came. It is not common for someone in Mussoorie to move abroad to pursue a master's. My didi will continue to be a town role model for months to come. Even the *panwaadi bhaiya* on Mall Road knows about Riti Didi going abroad.

'I'm sorry if I am late,' Nishit said as I received him at the main gate.

'Oh no, you've made it just in time,' I smiled.

'Wow, the entire lawn has been done up in white and fairy lights. It looks like a beautiful party,' Nishit exclaimed.

'Oh yes! We're going to have a good time,' I winked.

I introduced Nishit to a couple of people before Shelly arrived. When Shelly joined us, the first thing she said was, 'Let us get a drink from the bar.'

'Shelly, not today, please,' I whispered while signalling her to keep her voice down.

But I knew that Shelly always does what her heart pleases. I would have to keep a check on her during the party so she didn't slip.

Nigam Uncle, who is one of our neighbours, walked up to us and said, 'We're all so proud of Riti. She has always been a bright kid.'

'Riti Didi is just amazing,' I said.

'I have seen the two of you hang out near Mall Road. My office is on the road that leads to Lal Tibba,' he said as he pointed at me and then Nishit. His eyebrows were raised in quite a knowing way.

'Nishit has asthma. He has been advised by doctors to take long walks on a daily basis,' Shelly interrupted. 'I accompany them on most occasions, my mom says it's healthy to walk 10,000 steps every day.'

Shelly has a habit of covering up for her friends whenever need be. She is the smartest one of us and has a way with words. She is the kind of friend each one of us needs in life to survive the harshest of people and their rudest remarks. She isn't afraid of anyone. She always stands by us.

There was an awkward silence. The next thing we knew was that Nigam Uncle had walked away to attack the spring rolls.

'Shelly you were too good,' Nishit said as he high-fived Shelly.

'Oh yes!' I said.

'Come on, let us try drinking,' Shelly said as she laughed.

'Shelly, we can't. It is illegal. We are not adults, okay?' I said as I made it clear that we were definitely not going to drink in my home.

So, diary, here's the thing. A lot of our classmates have started experimenting with drinking and having sex because they feel they're almost adults. There is a newfound air of freedom in most of the people of our age. I don't know whether it is because we are bubbling with the energy of the hormones that are at play in our bodies or if we are just fighting a society that psychologically binds us to abstain from these acts until we have physiologically attained a particular age.

All I know is that everyone wants to be a rebel without an actual cause.

Mom dragged me along with her to meet her friends from the colony kitty party circle. I wanted to avoid those aunties because they are even worse than Nigam Uncle in digging out information. They have all the information they're not supposed to have. They just don't mind their own business.

And then, I saw Riti Didi speaking with Anuv. Riti Didi tells me everything about her life. I do the same. Do you remember, diary?

I told you that she knows about Nishit and my relationship. Well, I know about hers too. Anuv is her boyfriend.

They were engaged in an animated conversation.

How hard it will be for both of them to continue with a long-distance relationship. Will it even work? It probably won't.

That's another reason why I have nightmares when I think about Nishit and I parting ways. Will it be easy? Will it be hard?

Will we stay together, forever? Will we never be together?

I don't know the answers to these questions yet. The only thing I know is that, my diary, you'll always be with me no matter where I am!

My reverie was broken as Nishit held my hand. 'Let's go to the terrace,' he said.

'Don't hold my hand publicly. There are spy aunties all around,' I said as I pulled my hand away and started to walk slowly towards the terrace. He followed me.

We sat on top of the water tank, which is a floor higher than the terrace and shadowed by trees. We looked at the party going on in the front lawn, as if we were watching a movie from a distance. Neither one of us spoke for a while.

'Not many months from now, it will be our farewell, at school, and at home too,' he broke the silence.

I placed my index finger on his lips to stop him from speaking further.

We did not speak for another ten minutes. Tears rolled down our cheeks as both of us were aware that the future wasn't going to be very kind to us.

The future might not even hold a few moments together for us let alone the dream of spending our lives together. We did not look at each other but towards the unending hills that stretched till the end of sight. We could see the lights from some beautiful Garhwali homes and temples twinkling in the faraway mountains, just like the stars in the sky above. It looked as if the landscape was a vast ocean acting like a mirror that reflected the twinkling lights of the stars above. A mirror image separated at the horizon.

'You'll look handsome in a suit. I look forward to gazing at you during our farewell,' I broke the silence that stretched to the hills.

'You'll look beautiful in a saree,' he smiled at me.

And then, for a change, we kept looking at each other. Maybe, an hour went by. Maybe, it was less than that.

Then my dad started singing 'Papa Kehte Hai Bada Naam Karegi' on the karaoke machine. He had practised that song for a week. You know how much he loves physics and music. That was my cue to return to the party as it would have been hard to go unnoticed any longer. The act involved me getting on the stage and dancing with Dad.

I told Nishit we had to go back, and I made it on to the stage just in time. Then, we all danced like there was no tomorrow. I knew it was one of the last few parties in Mussoorie where all my near and dear ones would gather.

Last night, I danced like I did not care about the future.

Cheerio,

Iti

The Terrace—2

20 May 2020

Dear Diary,

The last few weeks have turned out to be the most eventful weeks of my life.

I can't believe that I mustered the courage to read my diary from the year when I lost my family. That was the worst year of my life.

A few days ago, as I was sifting through old photographs with Shyamala Aunty, I discovered my first-ever passport-size picture, which was pasted on my school identity card. We are working on an interesting project, collecting not just photographs but defining moments and stories from our family's past. These moments, happy or sad, define our lives through the years.

We've lost precious people along the way while others have become a part of this journey. It made me reflect and introspect on the term 'identity'.

My identity has kept evolving over the years, however, I've mostly been identified via my identity cards. First school, then college, then my job, and oh yes, my passports, tax return slips, and my Aadhaar too. While all these capture some parts of my identity, I feel that none has been able to capture it in its absolute sense.

Maybe, even my identity isn't absolute, like the universe, ever-changing and ever-evolving.

Why do so many of us resort to labels and identities, and the stereotypes that come with them? 'She's white, he's black.' This sentence has four words and on reading it each person would identify with something.

We say let's accept our differences. I question why we created separate identities in the first place. Isn't being a human identity enough? Just like the elements in the periodic table. Or just like a dog that recognizes a human without knowing their name. Or a bird that recognizes a fellow bird. It could be a crazy thought, but I've been thinking a lot of crazy things these days.

While on some days I question my lost identity, on other days I question the identity I wish to maintain in the present.

A strange thought did come to me today. The universe is infinite, but we're limited by our thoughts and therefore caged. You can be free but trapped, and trapped but free.

Sometimes, thinking a lot just complicates things. Life progresses just like your years in college. Your first year might feel like the worst thing that has ever happened to you, while your last year was so good that you cling to it forever. At least in your memories.

I moved out of my room to write on the terrace today. I am writing from every corner of this house. The terrace has always been special.

The green muffler has worked. Nishit came to meet me today. I had also invited Shelly over. It is time to act mature. It is time to make amends.

They both got to my house at the same time. It was funny to me that while I had invited both of them separately, they had somehow turned up together. God knows how they always managed to do this. I always thought they knew how to practice telepathy.

They had seemingly moved on. I got that feeling when I met Nishit in the park and then Shelly in the store.

They seemed to have forgiven me and moved on long ago. It is stupid me who has been cursing them all along and staying bitter. I wish I could have forgiven and forgotten long ago too, but I guess I didn't because I was always the dumbest of the three of us.

We chatted about everything and anything.

I learnt that Nishit is engaged now. It somehow did not bother me as long as we could patch up as friends.

Nishit learnt what had happened between Shelly and me. He never knew the truth.

I think Shelly has forgiven me for what I did to her in school. That rumour I had started about her being a lesbian had impacted her reputation so much that she had had to leave town. She did mention to me the hardships she had had to go through because of the rumour, which had gone around the school like wildfire.

They realized that I had lost my entire family in a car accident.

Life has come full circle this year. I also told them about my new story idea and that it has a happy ending since my boss Kajol Sir wanted a feel-good story. I told them about the characters that were based on them, and how my script gave me a chance to manipulate reality. They laughed and laughed about it. They claimed they would never befriend a writer again for fear of ending up as the characters in her stories.

We chatted and laughed for hours. It felt like home. It felt like the good old times when we were inseparable. While the world goes around and comes around for us, the terrace will always be our place. It will always be the place where the sun never sets for us.

It is funny that when you're a child all you want is to grow up. And when you grow up you realize how stupid you were. Ironic, but it's the hard truth.

I told them that the sky looked wonderful, and I wanted a few minutes to just gaze at it. I pondered that the biggest lesson the lockdown had taught us was the importance of our loved ones. The value of being grateful for the small things in life. The feeling of appreciation for anything and everything human.

As I gazed at the stars, I felt at complete ease in that moment. They joined me. None of us moved, even a bit. We had a friendship like the stars in a constellation that never change their relative position.

Then, I opened up to them about the greatest regret of my life. I don't know why, but I have not mustered enough courage to share this even with you. But as they say, the magic of best friends is above all.

I told them about the void that Jay has left in my life. Yes, my little brother Jay. I might not give him enough credit, but he was the joy of my life. Waking up to his adorable little face had always made my day. Jay was like my baby.

Always.

When Mom and Dad went off to work, they entrusted me with the job of feeding him and getting him ready for school. I was chosen by Dad to speak to Jay's school teachers and tutors on his behalf. I knew his biggest fears and even bigger dreams. He told me everything by writing it all down in a little blue diary he had.

It was so because Jay couldn't take a stand for himself. He was deaf and hence dumb. He went to a school for the specially-abled. But he was intelligent and supremely talented, with a brain like Dad's.

He would paint, and paint some more for hours. Mom had turned the outhouse into an exhibition space because we wanted to sell his paintings. We always validated his works of art in whichever way we could.

He was full of aspirations. He wanted to study physics at an Ivy League college and travel the world sharing his ideas.

Only the sky was the limit for him.

If he were alive during the lockdown, he would have evoked a sense of wonder in my life every day. Life without him is like a curry without salt. It is tasteless and hence senseless.

I told Nishit and Shelly how lucky they were to have a family in these times of lockdown. I did not have anyone except for Shyamala Aunty, who means family to me now.

Jay and I are soulmates no matter where we go in life. A part of him will always be alive in me. We don't have to talk every day. We never had to. We would stay silent for hours, yet we always felt complete. That's the kind of sense of belonging that I have not felt in years.

Shyamala Aunty broke my reflections as she came out to the terrace to serve us amazing food. She had prepared all our favourite dishes. She has known all of us for years and knows exactly what each one of us wants.

After spending hours getting dressed up to feed my ego and wanting to look gorgeous when I met Nishit again, I realized that slipping my pyjamas on was the best part of my day.

After Nishit and Shelly left, I sat and wrote at the speed that a jet flies.

I finally completed my script. Shyamala Aunty smiled every time she came into my room to give me food or ask me if I wanted coffee.

Aren't the best trips the unplanned ones? Aren't the mornings after the nights of long conversations with a bunch of friends the best ones? Don't we look the most beautiful when we don't have time to get dressed up and wear make-up as we haven't slept much the last night?

But only two days ago the peace of my solitude was broken. We received an email that we need to be back in Gurgaon in June. That we need to present our ideas for a movie script as a pitch presentation in person to our seniors and the newly appointed team at Lightspeed productions.

This week was so eventful that I did not get a chance to share all these big developments with you. I hope you will forgive me. Will you?

My movie ought to be a super hit. It is now exactly the story of my life. It also has a feel-good friends' reunion in times of lockdown. It is the story that Kajol Sir wanted. This time I have followed Shyamala Aunty's and everyone else's suggestion of writing a relatable story about my own life.

I can't wait for my idea to be approved and made into a film.

Yours truly,

Iti

The New Normal

21 June 2020

Dear Diary,

Today was my first day in the city after months of living in my hometown.

The other half of 2020, also known as the 'new normal', doesn't feel good. It just feels like settling for less than what you imagined for your future. I had always imagined spending more time with my friends when I got my first job because then I'd have the money to afford all the expensive places. I could take them out for brunches and dinners!

Can you ever plan life? Most certainly, no. It just happens, as the magic unfurls. Or, it's mostly a disaster.

The new normal meant no promotion and a salary cut. All you had to be thankful for was not being fired from your company because that was the fate of thousands. You had to tell yourself that you're lucky and you had to settle. You had to be thankful that you don't need Soni Mahajan to get you a job. By the way, Soni Mahajan is the coolest actress on social media. She has left acting and has ventured into the humanitarian cause of finding work for the jobless during the pandemic. You just tweet her and she helps you find a job.

We all think we control our lives. We believe that time and again. And if we feel that the steering wheel isn't in our hands we rely on God. But 2020 has been living proof that maybe we are not in control of our lives. Perhaps we never were! 2020 is more like an alarm you can't snooze. You have to wake up.

This reminded me of an ex-colleague of mine, Shankar, who once told me that I must learn to drive. He could not digest the fact that I could row a canoe but couldn't drive.

I told him, 'I never thought that luxury was about being able to afford the latest car. I always thought that luxury was about being able to afford a chauffeur. While buying a luxury car would mean feeding some European or American multinational company that is already obese enough, hiring a driver would mean generating some employment and sharing the wealth with the needy.' One has to think differently when we live in a developing country run by relentless advertisers like me.

I offered another point to counter his insistence that I learn how to drive. And this had nothing to do with reviving the economy of India. It was about the future. I told him, 'Companies like Tesla have already come up with self-driving cars. Why should one move towards the past? Shouldn't we move towards the future?'

Much to my surprise, he had a counter-argument. He said, 'Driving a car that runs on autopilot means you'd be relinquishing control. Wouldn't it be scary if your life was not in your control?'

I laughed. And laughed. And laughed. I told him, 'Modern jets fly mostly on autopilot. When they're not, they're still being navigated by some human pilot who is busy clicking pictures for his influencer account. You're already relinquishing control. Doesn't that scare you?'

He had yet another counterpoint. You know, men hate to lose an argument! He said, 'You take a flight twice a year but you drive the car every day.'

I laughed again. It has always baffled me how some people have such a myopic view of the world. They never look at all the aspects of something before coming to a conclusion. I reminded him, 'Your mother takes a metro train to work every day and metro trains run quite like modern jets: half man, half machine.'

We kept talking for hours and never concluded the argument because he was adamant about his point of view. He wanted to win. I wanted a better solution. I also just wanted to pass time, neither win nor lose.

Finally, I told him, 'I will learn how to drive.'

For me, it was never about winning the argument over whether I should learn to drive or not. I wanted to come up with plenty of options. I never knew that I would be able to view the situation through so many lenses.

But let me warn you. If you want to please everyone you can't have a point of view or an opinion. Because the moment you start to have an opinion, you'll be at loggerheads with people who have a counter-opinion. As children, we're free of prejudice and that's why we bond well with our grandparents. Whereas our parents may have a different outlook on life and therefore are in an undeclared cold war with our grandparents.

But should we cease to have an opinion in the first place? No! We must always have an opinion. Knowing what you stand for is always important in life.

I am a writer at heart, you see. I have to do this kind of thing. That's how I earn my bread and butter. But that is also how I am supposed to come up with better solutions for society. I don't wish to write erotica and die. I wish to leave an impact on society. Not that I don't agree with people having better sex; but I also want them to focus on creating progeny who make the world a better place.

But why am I writing about it today? I remember that discussion vividly because somewhere along the way it was no longer about whether one should learn to drive or not. It was about winning and losing for him. While for me, it was about control.

Don't we all want to be in control of our lives, diary? But are we? Really?

The 'new normal' is proof that you can't always plan the future. I used to firmly believe that everything was under my control, but the 'new normal' seems to challenge the notion that we can always plan the future. Control has slipped from our hands like smooth beach sand.

As if the threat of nuclear war wasn't enough to scare our grandparents, God planned Covid-19 to scare us. Now, time is divided, pre and post Covid-19. While the time period of the pandemic stands separate, a hazy bubble of isolation. You were jailed for not committing any crime.

The world was locked up.

Mankind had deemed itself far more powerful than it is. That's why we were presented with this divine wake-up call.

I don't believe in God as religions dictate. I believe in God as a being representing all that's not under my control—that is beyond my understanding. I don't believe you have to blindly worship some men who may have existed in history. They could also be a figment of some writer's imagination.

Writers make up characters all the time. Many years later, blogger Ramy of the iconic blog 'On the Open Road' may become God. I feel the only way to meet God is by embarking on the journey of knowledge and wisdom. The only worship would be to realize one's karma.

The new normal, the new agonizing reality, gave me all the reasons to be able to reach God. Finishing this movie script, writing it through the lockdown, allowed me to identify my karma.

Now, there's no looking back. I feel I am born to do this. I have embarked on this journey of writing. I will keep moving on and come up with many scripts until I die. Probably, that's the reason death did not take me when I wanted it to.

These thoughts flashed through my mind as I drove to my office in Gurgaon after months of working from my home in Mussoorie. You see, I did learn how to drive!

And I did tell Riddhima on the way back that I had lost my family long ago. She was taken aback to learn that I had spent one of the most daunting times in the history of humanity without family. It made her show sympathy for three minutes and then she was back to normal.

Today, either my work would be validated or trashed. Prakash Sir would finalize which script went into production and finally became a film. Riddhima would have given her best try, as would my other colleagues.

Nevertheless, 2020 had a lot to teach us. It can be said that life came full circle this year. I was certainly grateful for the small things in life. While all through my life happiness meant a holiday abroad, now even being able to drive to the office made me feel happy. Blissful. Content. 'Driving' and 'office' had been my all-time least-preferred things!

It reminded me of Dad, who always told me, 'Time is the most important variable and change is the only constant.'

As a human, you are ever-changing, ever-evolving. I certainly appreciate the things in my life that I had taken for granted. It did not happen overnight. It certainly took me an entire lockdown and isolation to realize that.

Has it ever happened to you that the person you help does better than you? Has it ever happened to you that you lost a job or failed an exam because you could not make it in time due to traffic? Again. Something that is not under your control.

Riddhima told me on the drive back home that her story was a drama based on a Bollywood film star Shashwat's death back in May under mysterious circumstances. The media is raging about his girlfriend Miha and her role in abetting his suicide.

I quite liked her idea.

You won't believe me, my diary, they picked Siddharth's stupid movie script over either of our scripts. In fact, he stole Riddhima's idea.

They justified the choice by saying that everyone wants to watch a biopic these days. Nobody cares about fiction anymore.

They chose Siddharth's script over Riddhima's because gender inequality is the reality of our corporate towers.

I resigned from the company. Before I left I told them, 'I am going to tell every girl to rise and shine because these words are rarely said to us in the course of our lives. Instead, we're told to adjust in life by compromising in relationships, by giving up education and careers, by dressing and sitting in a certain way, by settling for being the last person to join the dinner table after the men are done relishing hot chapatis. Dear seniors, please do not treat us like goddesses or princesses on Women's Day, just treat us as equals on the rest of the days if you can.'

I congratulated Siddharth before I walked out confidently and pressed the call button for the lift. I was so sure about my story that even though it had failed to be selected at Lightspeed I knew it could be transformed into a movie by a better production company. When life closes a door someplace it opens other doors in other places. It is just about taking the time to see and find those doors.

The time I have spent in reflection and the amends that I have made in my life have changed me as a person.

And I am loving this new person that I have become. I am at ease with myself. I am finally a writer who doesn't care about being accepted or rejected by society. I am finally someone who finds pleasure in this journey of life.

I did not die because I am yet to realize my karma.

Always,
Iti

Epilogue

1 January 2022

Movie Premiere

The theatre was full. Everyone was wearing a mask. If you lived post-2020 you knew that masks were as important as your socks and underwear. We live in a country where a girl could wink and move the nation. This was bigger than that.

Life was not the same.

Shyamala Aunty was so excited. She had taken a flight for the first time. Her kids were so spellbound, they were dancing all over the theatre. Shyamala Aunty is super proud of me. And she had to come today. She is like my mother, my biggest support system to date.

It is strange how we define family by blood ties and often fail to be grateful for people who become more than family despite having no blood ties to us.

I had the feeling one gets before writing an exam. Butterflies, butterflies and some more butterflies.

Oh! So did I forget to mention, readers?

My movie *Where the Sun Never Sets* premiered in India today as the lockdown norms have been relaxed. It was so loved by the producers who bought the rights that we showcased it online last month at the South Asian film festival. The movie has been doing superbly for the past month all over Southeast Asia on an established OTT platform.

I do hope that wherever Nishit and Shelly are, they get to see the film. By the way, don't be surprised, but I have not met them for several years now.

Now you must be wondering what actually happened? What is the true story?

Here's the fact check just in case you're becoming impatient and want to kill me for making you believe my story. But I did warn you about reading my diary in the beginning, didn't I?

Everything I wrote in this diary and that you've read is the final script of my film. Please don't get angry at me. I had warned you at the beginning that I am a deadly combination. I am an advertising professional who conveniently sells lies and I am a super storyteller too.

Now you must be wondering if I lied about my family too. No, I didn't. I wish they were here to see this day. They would have been super proud of me.

But I did lose them to a car accident in 2016.

I formally introduced Shyamala Aunty on stage. Everyone recognized her character from the movie. She walked on to the stage and she said, 'Iti was so dedicated that she did not move out of her room even once during the lockdown so she could finish her movie script.'

The audience went berserk over the story. They hooted and clapped like crazies and validated my dream career. You should have seen my face, I could not be happier.

We enjoyed the premiere as I got to meet the producers who now want to sign me up as the scriptwriter for their pipeline projects.

As the night drew to a close, I finally turned my smartphone on after months of being too wired up by the process of finishing my dream movie script to check social media.

The first thing I did was to stalk Nishit and Shelly on Facebook. I wanted to make amends, like the movie script that had a happy ending. I had finally found my closure.

And you won't believe this, but right when I was doing this in my car, I received a call from an unknown number. Telepathy is real, I guess.

'Hello,' I said, curious.

'Congratulations, Iti!' It was Shelly on the other side.

'Thanks,' I replied. I was happy that my best friends did get a chance to see my version of our story.

'Do you recognize me?' she asked me as she wasn't sure if I did recognize her voice or if I was just acting smart by saying thank you as we do on so many occasions.

'Yes, of course, Shelly.' I added, 'How have you been? How is Nishit doing?'

'We are doing fine.'

'Where are you guys these days?'

'We are in northern Norway. We are celebrating our anniversary here as the lockdown norms have been relaxed a bit. Nishit is back to flying for Lufthansa.'

'Oh wow! Did you go check out the place? Where the sun never sets?' I said with a smile, although it hurt like a nail that had pierced right through my heart.

'Oh yes. We did. Coincidentally, we also watched your film last night.'

'Did you guys like it?' I enquired yet again like a delivery agent who won't go until you've proven that the package belongs to you.

'Oh! We loved it.'

'I am glad you did,' I tried to end the conversation. I wanted to know more, but at the same time, I did not want to know so much as to feel upset.

'You've made us Nihaal and Molly, I suppose?' she asked.

'Yes.'

'When did I kiss you?' She asked me just when I felt that I wasn't prepared to face the hard questions about my version of the story.

'You didn't. But I couldn't digest the fact that you and Nishit kissed when we were in school. When I went back home, I wanted to believe in my version of the story, and I wrote the diary entry accordingly. When I rediscovered the diary in Mussoorie and started to base my movie plot on my diary entries I chose to keep my versions of the story rather than the facts. The movie is a work of fiction. It is inspired by true events. It is not a hundred per cent true story.'

'I loved the ending though,' she emphasized.

'You did? Molly and Nihaal don't get married at the end of my story, Smiti and Nihaal do. I chose the ending the way I wanted it to be back in school,' I said.

'Of course, we did like your ending. We did not do the best thing to you. And we were sorry back in school, and we are still sorry,' she said then added, 'You said that we are soulmates at the end of the film, the three of us. It means a lot to us after all that we did to you. Have you forgiven us?'

'It's okay, Shelly. I am happy that you guys are happy. I have moved past the fact that you guys cheated on me. I have forgiven you,' I assured her as tears rolled down my cheeks.

'Thank you for forgiving us,' Shelly said, sounding unconvinced but hopeful.

'That's the positive thing about being a storyteller. I will always have my version of the story. I am free to believe in whatever it is that I want to believe,' I said.

'Let's meet sometime?' she asked.

'Ring me up when you guys are in India,' I said.

'By the time we get to India you'll get to meet Nishit junior too,' she chirped.

'Oh! Congratulations. I am so happy for you two. May God bless the baby,' I couldn't say much more. I hung up.

I wish Nishit had spoken to me to congratulate me too. Why was Shelly speaking on 'their' behalf? I guess that is how it happens with married couples.

Nishit was the only love of my life. Tears rolled down my cheeks as I placed the phone in my purse. I started the car engine. I decided to go on a drive alone before I came back to pick up Shyamala Aunty and the kids to finally leave for the hotel where we'd booked our stay.

'You must get married to a suitable boy, Iti. I can't look after you forever,' Shyamala Aunty said later as we drove to the hotel.

'My stories are my true soulmates. As long as I write I will be able to find hope in the darkest of times. Maybe God sent me on earth for this,' I said.

'Iti, you have your fundas! Your uncle Nick had a similar outlook on life. Are all creative geniuses crazy?' she pondered.

'You know what Shyamala Aunty? While people will come and go in my life, my stories will stay with me forever. My passion is my only hope to survive,' I tried to make her understand. I knew though that it would be unfathomable to her.

'What happened to them in real life?' Shyamala Aunty enquired.

'Who?' I acted as if I did not know who she was referring to.

'Shelly and Nishit, beta. In your movie, Smiti gets married to Nihaal. But I see that you are still single. Where is Nihaal?'

'They are happily married to each other, Nihaal and Molly, I mean Nishit and Shelly,' I muttered.

'Why did you spread the rumour about Shelly in school?'

'I was immature and young. I couldn't believe that they had cheated on me. I was furious. I couldn't hurt Nishit despite what he did to me. I was madly in love with him. On the other hand, Shelly was my best friend. I had never expected her to do this to me. So that rumour about her kissing me was my immature revenge to settle scores,' I explained.

'Have you forgiven them now?'

'Yes. I have moved on. Writing this script helped me find closure. It helped me heal.'

'Will you meet them?' she asked.

'Maybe yes, maybe no!' I replied.

I posted my picture from the premiere on Instagram. I captioned it, 'Fiction has the power to move people through the magic one can weave using words. Reality is incomplete without a dash of fiction. A cat has nine lives, but a writer lives many!'

Surprisingly, Riti Didi commented, 'I am proud of you, bachcha! See you soon in India.' She then sent me a WhatsApp text that read: Don't think you're safe kiddo! I'm coming home later this month to steal your passwords, expose your boyfriends, eat your portion of chocolates, break your gadgets, unearth your beer bottles, hack your room and simply annoy you in every possible way. Just because I got married to Patrick doesn't mean I cease to exist.

'Riti is married too,' I said to Shyamala Aunty.

We both looked at each other and laughed.

After many quarrels, pillow fights, chappal wars and thrashings by parents, we were going to be the great Indian inseparable siblings now. I have forgiven Riti Didi too.

My movie helped me bring the people I had lost back into my life. I had never shared my problems and therefore the problems never went away.

Poonam Malwani, my therapist, had always told me that communication is the basis of strong relationships. You can't keep expecting things from people without communicating what you want.

My movie sent my heart's message to the people I loved.

Now, people love me based on my talent and not those imperfect outward appearances. They see the beauty within me. They see that beauty can be radiated from the inside of a human spirit. They feel I'm beautiful because I feel that I'm beautiful. I'm confident, talented and unstoppable.

As a teenager, I never imagined that I could have a boyfriend, let alone the fan following that I have now! Be you. Be real. That's the best you can ever be. Life isn't perfect. It is like the last page of your notebook. Erratic. Yet it is one of the best pages that has numerous stories to tell.

Whenever I travel to places, I relive moments from the books that I've read. And sometimes, I wish to recreate them for my readers, who will probably read them even years after I die.

On the night of the movie premiere, my younger self visited me in my dreams. It was a surreal experience.

She asked me, 'How are you?'

I told her, 'I have never been this happy in my entire life.'

She laughed hard, 'What took you so long?' I stared into her eyes. I had no answer.

Then I blurted out, 'Good things have been happening to me of late. Maybe it's luck or a jackpot that I have landed upon.'

She laughed and said, 'I don't think so. You're still a writer. You still work from random places. You still don't have a family. Same old, same old. Not much has changed around you. It's the same old life you've been living all along.'

I realized that she was spot on. Nothing had changed in my life except for the fact that I had changed from within.

I believe that this life is precious and these moments are almost like a second chance. My perspectives have evolved. My spiritual inclination has changed. My love for myself is so much that I'm borderline narcissistic. Just saying, not really.

But before I could say this to the younger me, she vanished. And I woke up from my dream in the middle of the night.

Maybe that was an inner realization that I have subconsciously had for a few weeks but it hit me all at once last night. While I have so many answers to find in this journey of life, I have finally found the answer to this tough question about life: How can one chase happiness in life? It might sound counterintuitive, but I can share from my experience that it's the other way round. You need to change yourself from within and happiness will chase you forever.

We consume a lot of fiction day in and out, more so in the times of the pandemic when movement for most of us has been restricted like never before, and we are looking for an alternative way to experience the world outside. Being a writer, I consume content in numerous forms—books, audio, video and whatnot.

While fiction serves as a momentary escape from real life for most of us, sometimes, it also inspires us to become a better version of ourselves as we step into our favourite character's shoes. This is the kind of positive impact that fiction must have.

I hope that this story does that for you.

Often, we become so obsessed with the fictional content out there that we start finding gaps in our real life, unable to stay happy anymore.

It's important to take inspiration from fictional stories but equally important to remember that sometimes real life is complex and comes with its own set of unique challenges that can't be compared to any fictional situation.

The next time you meet someone, don't ask 'How are you?' but 'How are you feeling?' instead. And if you're not feeling okay, talk to someone you trust. Talk! It's time we talk about being mentally fit as much as we talk about being physically fit. In my opinion, it's okay not to feel okay on some days. A perfect life is an illusion. A happy ending is just a story.

Life is challenging, dark and grim sometimes. But there's light at the end of the tunnel. When we look at people, in person or on social media, all we see is what they want to show. That doesn't necessarily mean that it's a true reflection of their inner self. There's a storm going on in everyone's mind. Be kind. Be gentle.

Be empathetic. That's the best we can do at a personal level to bring about change.

I now live in my family home with Shyamala Aunty and her kids in the queen of the hills Mussoorie where the mornings sing and the evenings dance! I am a full-time writer. I am home.

Afterword

Life is too short.

Call up that friend you have not spoken to for months! Call up that family member who broke your heart!

Maybe it is time that you call up your Riti, Nishit and Shelly. Maybe head out on a road trip with them.

For life is precious and the people close to us are priceless. Don't let the pain of the past stop you from building a beautiful future.

The bird in you should find its way back home, sooner or later.

Feeling Inspired?

MAKE A MOVE. Start your journey into the remarkable today.

Do give my books *On the Open Road* and *You Only Live Once* a read. I promise that they will inspire you as much as this one, as much as they inspired many readers.

Please leave a review on Amazon and Goodreads. It will help me reach out to more readers who can be inspired to touch people's lives with their ideas!

If you'd like, also share your thoughts on social media using #stutichangle, #SCFamily. I call my readers #SCFamily.